I0582827

Second Hand Murder

A thrilling, race-against-the-clock
cozy mystery
Christa Bakker

Counting Blessings

Contents

1

Are you safe?

'Are you safe?'

Franck's words hung in the air and seemed to echo around me. Was I safe? I thought I was. But then why would he ask me that? That all too familiar feeling of unease crept up on me again.

Where was Franck? He'd asked the words, but I couldn't see him. I was in some sort of room, but everything was a blurry, soft yellow. Where was I? *Was* I safe? I didn't know! I needed to get to Franck. He'd keep me safe. But where was he?

'Franck!'

Drenched in cold sweat, I opened my eyes to see the early morning light peeping through the gap between the shutters. The alarm on my smartwatch was angrily buzzing at me, but I could kiss it! Four years, five months, and three days of freedom from that man, and he still haunted my dreams. They'd only got worse after he was released from prison, now five months ago. I'd expected my criminal ex-husband to make good on his death threat, but any threatening thing that had happened in those months could have been explained by my overly suspicious mind playing tricks on me.

I turned to lie on my back and spread out to cool off. The day hadn't even started, and I was already hot. I should probably open the shutters now and let the air in before it warmed up even more. I'd set my alarm for half past five, so the sun wouldn't be fully up for another hour. What was I thinking, agreeing to help Céline out with this *vide-grenier*? I knew second-hand markets started in the middle of the night. Had I lost my mind?

I stretched, still unable to shake the fear generated by my dream, which had been part memory. Franck had asked me whether I was safe so many times. At first, I'd thought it was sweet, that he was being protective. Then I'd started to wonder.

Remember, we're out this afternoon. Were we? He'd ask me if I'd forgotten again. *Now*, of course, I knew there was nothing wrong with me. That he'd been messing with my head all that time, and for what? Just so he could feel more in control. Well, I'd taken all control away from him.

Despite the heatwave, I shivered. Prison couldn't have changed him so much that he would have forgiven me that. But not even my assistant Thibault, who was his nephew, had mentioned him in the past few weeks. Franck was just... there, in the background of my life, quietly threatening to make good on his promise to end my life.

I pressed my palms to my eyes and repeated my mantra. *I am a strong woman and I won't let Franck rule my life any more.* It took a few moments for my body and my mind to believe it after the dream I'd had, but when the truth of my mantra had settled in, I slapped my hands to the bed sheets either side of me and jumped out of bed. I *was* a strong woman. Even early in the morning at five – I checked my watch – fifty! Céline would be here any moment now and I wasn't even dressed.

Throwing on a light summer dress and hiding my unkempt hair under a scarf, I just had time to enhance my face with some nice lashes before I heard a car pull up. Wedge espadrille sandals in hand, I raced downstairs, where Thibault was already stacking boxes.

'Beau? Aren't you supposed to be asleep?'

'Good morning, boss,' he said pointedly, his muscles flexing as he lifted another box.

I cocked my head. 'Can you maybe unbutton that shirt, and I'll go get my camera?' Why should pin-ups be just women?

Beau put the box down with a little too much force. Behind his back, Céline came into the room with her phone held high in front of her face. She'd obviously heard my remark.

'May I remind you once again that I'm your assistant, not your subject?' Beau grumbled, his voice not used to performing this early. After that one disastrous attempt, I had no intention of ever trying to do a shoot with him again, but I couldn't help teasing him about it.

'Aww, so I have to delete my pics?' Céline asked. 'They would look better if you'd get... just this one...' She wrapped her arms around his chest from behind and reached for his top button. Poor Beau, who'd carried a torch for her for years but was thoroughly friend-zoned, could only close his eyes for a moment before his mask slid into place and he made a light-hearted swat at her hand.

'Get off me! Find someone else to undress.' He crossed his arms, and Céline and I both enjoyed the view.

'Or what?' She rubbed her shoulder against his arm. 'You're going back to bed? All nice and snuggly?'

Beau gave her a mock glare but pointed his finger at me. 'You're a bad influence. This used to be a sweet, innocent girl. Now look at her.' He turned her by her shoulders and marched her out the door, picking up one of the boxes on the way.

To me, Céline still looked like a sweet, innocent girl. But they were almost ten years younger than me, and those years seemed to really count. Had I been as sweet and innocent as that ten years ago? I shook my head and slipped on my shoes. Even Céline was getting more flirty. Though she'd broken up with her boyfriend, he must have changed her in some way.

I sighed and went to close one of the boxes that was still open. I was supposed to have closed them all up last night, but I'd got stuck in a nostalgic mood. Most of what was in these boxes had belonged to my great-aunt Géraldine, who'd passed away some months before. My house used to be hers, and she'd signed it over to me on condition of me keeping some of her things for her. She'd said it was for when she'd return, even though she loved the assisted-living facility she'd had to retreat to. Now, it was time to let go of her things, but last night, after a glass of wine or two, I'd almost called the whole thing off.

I winked at the ugly clown candlestick holder in the box, sent Aunt Géraldine a mental kiss, and taped up the box. This morning, the whole lot could go. I'd have my memories with or without this stuff, and perhaps it would help Céline raise some more money for charity. Whistling a popular tune, I picked up the box and brought it out to Céline's bakery van.

'You're in a good mood,' she commented with a smile. 'I wouldn't have taken you for an early riser.'

'I am a strong woman and I'm not going to let Franck rule my life any more,' I said without context.

Céline giggled. 'Good for you.'

But Beau looked up from packing. Ten months ago, he'd knocked on my door, asking for a place to stay. I'd wanted him gone ever since, but now I could see the moment of his leaving was coming – though I wasn't sure he even realised it himself –

I wasn't prepared for the melancholy that brought me. I'd once called him the spotted one in a family of black sheep. That still rung true. I wasn't sure what he was doing half the time and whether it was legal or not, but I'd come to think of him as *my* spotted sheep. My super fluffy, cuddly sheep with a blue bow around his neck.

My blurred gaze focused to show Beau frowning at me. I'd been staring at my sheep – assistant! – without realising it.

'Are you okay?'

I shook my head. 'Sorry, still half asleep.'

'Well, wake up. We're already behind.'

'Yes, boss.' I saluted him, then stuck out my tongue at his back, making Céline grin. He was right, though. Because of my nostalgia last night and my lateness this morning, we still had some packing and stacking to do when we should have been on our way to Villefranche, the city in the valley, a ten-minute drive from our village of Saint-Maurice.

Céline, the only one of us used to getting up early, chatted to us about other *vide-greniers* she'd been to. She liked collecting everyone's unwanted things to, as she put it, make sure they were wanted again. With a smile like hers, she could probably convince someone to even want my ugly clown candlestick holder. But I knew some of Aunt Géraldine's other stuff was actually valuable. I'd marked some antiques and pieces of art that my aunt had once told me were worth something so Céline wouldn't ask too little for them.

In a crate near the back of the van, I spotted some things from the village hotel I co-owned. My business partner, Jeanette Ta, had overseen the entire renovation and apparently decided these bits of seventies decor were never to grace our hotel again. I couldn't disagree. There were some mustard yellow and brown ceramic vases, a bulby, beige glass lampshade, and some paintings of Latina women and sad children. Céline would need all her powers of persuasion to shift those.

At twenty minutes past six, we finally shoved the last box into the van, and Céline drove us east into the valley. Seeing the sun rise above the city and over the vineyards around us was a sight I only experienced in winter, when it came at a time I was awake, but this was something else. Not the dark orange tones of winter, but an already bright yellow light lit up our faces and the whole Saône valley before us, all the way to the Alps in the far distance. Though Céline had to don her sunglasses and work the sun visor, I enjoyed every second of the silent beauty before me and was almost sad when we reached our destination.

August in France is the month everybody takes their holiday. Restaurants close – never mind the tourists – offices are empty, and even the strikers take a break. This August was no different, and with the heat added into the mix, anyone who hadn't left town was staying indoors. The streets of Villefranche were deserted.

'This is a good location,' Céline explained while we started unloading. 'It used to be an old market square before they built the school around it, so it has plenty of shaded spaces.' She unfolded a chair and put a pack of water bottles on top of it. Our trestle table was set up under an old, wooden structure that provided ample shade for about twenty other sellers. Not everyone was so lucky, though. Some tables were set up around the edge of the square, almost against the brick school wall. Some were still in its shade, but others were already heating up, the owners squinting into the light and wondering how long they'd last.

'Amateurs.' Céline winked at me. While other tables were a mess of random objects, she'd laid out a colourful tablecloth and was now arranging her wares in a haphazard, but optically pleasing way. As a photographer, I appreciated her effort, though I'd never seen this quality in her before. The window displays in the bakery were nice but not especially eye-catching.

As if she'd read my mind, Céline sighed. 'I can't wait to get my hands on our window. Dad won't let me touch it. He says the window display is a reflection of the baker, and he doesn't want it filled with bunnies and squirrels.'

Beau snorted. 'Does he think you are still eight years old?'

'Hey, I still like bunnies and squirrels. I just wouldn't put them in our window display, but try telling him that.'

We were only halfway through unpacking, but early punters were already lining up, some even checking in the van. Céline blocked their way. 'Sorry, you'll have to come back later or wait and check out my other wares.'

'You should have brought Frou-Frou to guard the van,' I said, knowing the little black Labrador would have been of no use at all.

Céline laughed. 'She is the girliest of dogs. Loves it when I put little pink bows in her fur.'

'It's because you named her Frou-Frou,' Beau said with disgust.

'She does her name proud. But she wants to be everyone's friend, so a guard dog, she is not. Besides, it would be cruel to have her out here in the heat once the day gets going.'

Part of me wanted to ask why it wasn't cruel for us to be out here, but then, we did make that insane choice ourselves. Henri, the stray cat who lived in my garden and sometimes in my house, hadn't shown himself in days. While Beau did most of the heavy lifting, Céline and I worked frantically to get everything out as quickly as we could. By the time we had everything set up, I was exhausted and sweating, but Céline had made a good number of sales already.

'Some of them are collectors and bargain hunters, but most are traders, looking for things to sell on.'

My gaze travelled over all the items still left on and around our table. 'My ugly clown is gone.'

'Are you kidding? That was the first thing to go. You may think it's ugly, but that was a highly collectable piece. Made the deaf children good money,' she said with a satisfied smile.

Her charity *du jour* was a nearby school for deaf children. Her trips to flea markets had already supported bread for people in South America, wounded wildlife in the Beaujolais, historical buildings in Villefranche, and women hoping to escape prostitution. Naturally, everyone was always happy to give her whatever she could find in their storage rooms.

Beau handed us both a bottle of water and took the last chair. 'Do you think we'll be busy today? With the heat and all?' he asked, taking a swig from his bottle and pulling his shirt away from his body.

A pleasant voice came from behind the table next to ours. 'Count on it.'

2

Why are you selling a basket of old keys?

The woman who owned the voice did not look like someone I would expect at a flea market. She was about my age, or perhaps slightly older, and immaculately dressed. Her outfit of an off-white linen top over linen trousers, paired with a slightly darker, long, gauzy blouse was so chic it made my mouth water. I'd already stolen glances at her table, which was covered with small stacks of antique lace. She'd arrived late as well, starting her set-up when we were unloading but finishing before we were done. But while I was fanning myself and trying not to look too hot and bothered, her tall, willowy figure exuded calm and elegance.

'Whenever I think nobody will come because of the weather, the real shoppers come out, thinking they'll try to score a bargain without too much competition. Before you know it, there's five people in front of you, all bidding for the same object. I'm Capucine, by the way.' She stretched out her hand and we all shook it. Her grip was firm and dry, unlike my sweaty palms. I was a strong, confident woman. But this one impressed me.

'Are you from Villefranche?' Beau asked, his most charming smile seeming to have no special effect on Capucine.

'I live on the outskirts. That long house with 1874 written in different coloured roof tiles? I suppose you won't know it unless you have business in Saint-Maurice.'

'Yes, we know that house,' Céline said. 'We're from Saint-Maurice, so we pass it all the time.'

Capucine was delighted and engaged Céline in a conversation on other *brocantes* she'd seen her at. Beau and I sat back a little, smiling at whoever came to our table, but mostly trying not to fall asleep. I kept myself awake by thinking about the champagne party I had planned for that afternoon. I'd invited all my previous clients for an intimate do, hoping they would all bring two friends who might also enjoy the experience of a cheeky vintage-style photoshoot with me. Why I had thought it a good idea to get up extra early on the same day and sit on a wooden chair for hours was beyond me now, but I'd made my bed and would have to lie in it. Mmm, bed...

'Coucou!' Jessica Rose waved her hand in front of me to take me out of my daydream. Her copper curls gleamed in the early morning sunlight, almost as brightly as her smile. 'Wake up! Not your usual time of day to be out, is it?'

I'd met Jessica when she saved me from destroying a priceless mural and had got to know her better when I consequently saved her from accusations of murder.

'No.' I had to clear my throat and repeat the word before it would come out. 'I'm only accompanying Céline.' Flapping my hand in Céline's direction, I woke up enough to manage a smile for Jessica and her millionaire boyfriend, Alain, who was browsing the wares. 'See anything you like?'

'Why are you selling a basket of old keys?' He held up an old padlock key with a mixture of curiosity and a degree of disgust on his handsome face.

'Ah. That. I'm already free, you see.' He did not see. How could he? I'd started that collection with the key to the house Franck and I had lived in. Truth be told, I stole it. Should have given it to the next tenant when Franck went to jail and I moved out, but that key was such an important symbol of my freedom that I couldn't let go of it. Some of the keys in that basket I'd found. Others I'd bought at flea markets such as this one. Some belonged to old diaries or the windows I'd replaced when I moved into Aunt Géraldine's house. Some keys came with stories, others were just part of the collection.

When Franck was released from prison a few months ago, I'd buried both my hands in the basket, wishing I could lock him up again. I'd stood there so long, my skin was dotted with little red marks made by the keys' ridges, but when I pulled my hands out of the basket, the keys had lost their magic. It was as if I'd drained them of both the negative and the positive power they'd once had on me. Franck had locked me up, but I had broken out. Then he was locked up, but now he was released. Somehow, it had all balanced out.

Yes, he'd threatened to kill me. But that was the old me, who was still under his influence. The me who'd let go of her family and friends because of him. Right now, I was the new me. The me I used to be before him, but now even stronger because of him. There were still moments like this morning when I had to repeat this to myself, but I didn't need the keys any more to remind me. And so, I'd packed them all up, even the pretty ones I'd framed and the little gold pendant Franck had once given me, and promised them to Céline and her worthy cause. The necklace had already sold, but the collection was still there.

'So how are you?' I asked Jessica so I wouldn't have to explain the whole thing. 'I haven't seen you in a while.'

Blushing, Jessica glanced at Alain. 'No, we... err... took a trip. Anaëlle – you remember her, right? – she took over the gallery and Alain had to help her with all the shady deals that came out of the woodwork. So when that was all fixed, Alain said he needed a break, and so we went, sort of, around the world.'

I grinned at her embarrassed happiness and she launched into an account of all the wonderful places she'd been and things she'd seen. For someone who'd started as a penniless kid from Marseille, she was doing the world's wonders proud, describing both ancient monuments and some Peruvian child's drawing with equal amounts of excitement. I sipped my water and thought that if I had to sit here and listen to her talk for another hour, it would be an hour well spent.

Unfortunately, Jessica had enough social sense to cut her story short. I made her promise to drop by for coffee at mine at some point so she could tell me more, and they moved on to Capucine's stall. Capucine greeted Alain by name, so I raised my eyebrows to Jessica. I'm not curious. It was a social nicety. But Jessica gave a discreet shrug. They'd only been together a few months. She couldn't have met all his acquaintances.

I couldn't wonder about it long, though, as the crowd was thickening, and I had to tend to punters interested in Aunt Géraldine's fruit bowl. As Capucine had predicted, almost everyone I talked to admitted they'd expected there to be fewer people around, but in the end, it was so busy that I didn't have a second to myself until about eleven o'clock, when the sun had got so strong that most shoppers went back to air conditioning and thick, old walls keeping the heat out.

I lowered myself gently onto the chair, ready to jump up and help more people, but Capucine laughed.

'No, that's it for now. You'll see that many sellers will pack up as well. I might do myself, actually. It's supposed to get even hotter than yesterday.'

I winced, thinking of all the champagne in my fridge. Would my guests let the weather stop them from coming? I checked my phone, but no cancellations had shown up yet. Of the sixteen people that were supposed to come, there were three who were the most likely to drop out on a day like this. My oldest client yet, a lady of eighty-six, was bringing two of her friends. I'd loved working with her, as she insisted I leave every wrinkle in the picture. Even in the ones showing her frilly pants, as per my whoops-did-my-skirt-just-fly-up style.

No ironing, or no money, she'd threatened. She didn't have to tell me twice. I keep things as natural as I can, because a woman's beauty is in her attitude. I want all my clients to have the confidence to show that beauty, no matter what they look like. If you've got it, own it. Whether it's orange peel skin or a pizza dough belly, you've lived your life long enough to get it, and that's worth something. Lady, you've earned that pizza dough!

Mind you, I didn't say flaunt it. That's a whole different story.

'Perhaps we should go too?' Céline raised her eyebrows at me.

I wasn't going to stand in the way of that. 'You're the boss. Have we sold enough?' I asked, more for politeness.

'Plenty.' She was already up and reaching for packing material. It seemed to me there was still a lot on our table, even valuable items. But Céline didn't give them a second thought, so I got up to help her pack up. Thibault had spotted a friend and was talking in a shady spot some distance away.

'Would you mind guarding my table for a minute so I can bring my car in?' Capucine asked Céline, who nodded. The *vide-grenier* was now almost deserted, and like Capucine had predicted, most sellers were starting to pack up.

Jessica appeared at our stall the moment Capucine had left. 'Alain says she's just an acquaintance. Apparently, her husband died rather unexpectedly. Thought you'd appreciate that little mystery.' She winked at me and hurried to join Alain, who waved in my direction.

I waved back, grinning when I caught Céline's concerned stare. 'Don't worry about it. Ever since I solved a few murders, people have exaggerated the circumstances of other people's deaths when talking to me. Invariably, these people weren't personally known to them. Capucine's husband probably just had a heart defect they hadn't known about, or something innocent like that. I'm only sorry she had to lose her husband at such a young age.'

My own father came to mind. He'd been forty-seven when he passed away. Since Capucine wasn't much older than me, her husband had probably been even younger. I hoped he hadn't left her with children who couldn't handle his death. I swallowed and decided to call my mother as soon as I got home.

'If you have no other plans for this afternoon,' I heard myself say when Capucine returned, 'I'm throwing a party for prospective clients. I know you're probably not that, but there will be champagne and a plethora of nibbles.'

Capucine raised both eyebrows, but after a moment's silence, said, 'Oh. Yes, that sounds lovely, actually.'

I gave her my address and the time, and continued wrapping objects in tissue paper. Though my invitation had been an impulse, I now rationalised that at least I wouldn't be stuck with too much champagne. Who knew? If she had money, she might even be tempted to book a shoot.

I closed a box and looked around for my assistant. Where had Beau got off to?

3

Keep an eye on Julie

Thibault winced as he motioned for the other man to join him elsewhere, out of sight of his companions. This whole thing had become far too complicated. When he agreed with Uncle Franck to keep an eye on Julie, it had all seemed fairly straightforward. It was already clear to the family that she hadn't found the key and wasn't looking for it, so she probably had no idea it existed. All Beau had to make sure of was that she didn't do 'anything silly', as Uncle Franck put it, as long as he was still in prison and unable to do anything about it.

At first, there wasn't much to do. Beau had been happy to see Julie slowly getting back on her feet, contacting family and old friends, and eventually starting a new business. She'd moved to a small flat and also rented a room she used as a studio, but both were in Villefranche and Beau had been quite bored with so little to do.

And then she moved to Saint-Maurice. Packed up all her things and left Villefranche to go back to the village where she'd grown up. Uncle Franck had been furious. Wasn't Beau supposed to keep an eye on her? Had he even made contact? Beau thought it prudent not to mention Uncle Franck had never instructed him to make contact. In fact, he'd said to make sure she wouldn't suspect a thing and it would be better to stay in the shadows.

Well, that's what Beau's family did best. Franck had stepped out of the shadows, and look what happened to him. Keep yourself hidden, unobtrusive, and you can do whatever you like. Beau had known about Julie's plans, of course. Keeping an eye on her had been the only task they'd trusted him with. They knew he liked her – much better than his own uncle – so they didn't put much faith in his loyalty to the family. But what other options did Beau have? Short of truly escaping and making a life somewhere far away, he was stuck. And not just because of his family...

Casting a quick glance at Céline, Thibault grabbed the man by his shirt. 'What are you doing here?' He forced himself to let go, in case Céline or Julie looked over their shoulder.

Quentin, one of his father's lesser minions, held his hands in front of his chest. 'She's getting rid of the keys.'

'And?'

'Well, obviously Franck wants to make sure—'

'You don't think I've checked them a hundred times over already? You can tell Uncle Franck that if this is how much he trusts me, he can do his own dirty work. I'm well over looking at wrinkly bums.'

Quentin grinned. 'Maybe he can send me in. I'll look at bums all day, even wrinkly ones.'

'Get lost.'

Stalking back to the table, Beau sighed. Quentin wasn't the worst. Most of the guys his dad employed weren't all that bad. Bit creepy, bit dodgy, with questionable morals, yes, but most of them just didn't know any better. If it hadn't been for his mother, Thibault himself probably would never have questioned the life his family led. But even though he did, he was still caught up in it. Much more than Julie realised.

'Ah, Beau, *tac*.' Julie dumped a heavy box in his arms, which he assumed he was to take to the van they'd parked outside the square.

'Thanks,' he snapped but refrained from further snarky remarks. He caught the look Céline and Julie shared and gritted his teeth while he left the square and headed for the van parked around the corner. Be affable. Play the good guy. Wasn't that what he'd been doing all along? He'd almost come to believe it at one point. How much easier would life be if he could just—

A sharp pain burst from the back of his head and shot into his shoulders, then his arms and his back. With a grunt, he sagged to his knees, dropping the box. But before he could hit the asphalt, strong arms grabbed him around his chest and dragged him off behind the van.

'Sorry, Beau, it had to look real. You wouldn't want this to happen to that sweet little girlie, right?' Alexis, Quentin's mate, did not sound sorry at all. He was taping Beau's hands behind his back, but at the half-threat to Céline, Beau lifted his aching head, fighting the stars. All he achieved by opening his mouth, however, was that Quentin had an easier time gagging him with some dirty cloth. He tried pushing it out with his tongue, but Alexis wrapped a bunch of tape around his head to secure the rag. He could only hope Julie would mind his hair when she took the tape off later.

Almost for show, he struggled against his bonds, but it only made the other two chuckle.

'You should know better than that, *mon gosse*. But don't worry, we're off now. We'll leave your little ladies alone. For now.'

Beau glared and grunted at them, but they left laughing, the cardboard box on one shoulder. He rested his head against the side of the van. At least he was in the shade, and it wouldn't be long until Julie or Céline found him. But Uncle Franck was getting more and more pushy. Beau got the feeling something new was up. Franck had to know the key wouldn't be in that box. Beau had searched the whole house top to bottom several times over. The key was not there.

Over the past nine months, Julie had come to trust Thibault. She'd let her guard down and confided in him on more than one occasion. He was absolutely sure she didn't know about the key. And yet, it wasn't where Uncle Franck had said he'd hidden it. So where was it?

Still, stealing that box now was idiotic. However many bad things Franck was, idiotic was not one of them. There had to be something else at play. To Franck, finding that key was essential, so in one way or another, the key was part of whatever else was going on. But by making it so obvious, even to Julie now, Franck was shining a light on actions he'd wanted hidden all this time. Why was it suddenly imperative that Julie knew about the key and knew that Franck was looking for it? What else was he planning?

A loud, high-pitched gasp made Beau look up into the glaring sunshine. Céline stood frozen with a box in her arms, staring at him. Julie came round the corner and bumped into her. Contrary to Céline, Julie immediately sprang into action, kneeling next to Beau to carefully undo the gag. Following Julie's lead, Céline then bent down to free Beau's arms.

The first thing he did when his hand was free was gingerly touch his head where Alexis had hit him. There was a bump the size of an egg, but at least the stars had disappeared.

'So?' Julie glared at him as if *he'd* done something wrong.

'What do you mean, "so"? These guys stole your box of stuff! What was in there, anyway?'

She looked confused. 'So you don't know who they were?'

Time for some more creative truths. 'Come on, Julie, really? It's not as if I know every petty criminal in Villefranche.' Close, but not quite.

Céline looked about to cry. Lying to her was a thousand times worse. Julie had got herself mixed up with Franck, but Céline was innocent. Wincing, he hauled himself up, leaning on the side of the van until he could see straight. Somehow, some time, he'd get back at Alexis for this.

Céline made a tiny bounce, then jumped into a hug, her arms around his neck. 'I'm so sorry!'

He wrapped his arms around her and never wanted to let go. Her body felt so good against his. He had to tell her none of this was her fault but selfishly, he wanted to delay the moment she'd pull back.

'It's not your fault,' he murmured instead into her hair. 'Not even one little bit.'

'How can you say that? I brought you here.' She pulled away slightly to look into his eyes.

Did she have to leave his arms so soon?

But then she reached out and touched the side of his face, his neck, his shoulder, his chest, every touch leaving a burning mark on his skin. 'Are you all right? Did they hurt you?'

'Calm down, *mon bébé*, I'm all right. It really isn't your responsibility when other people do bad things. Or even just stupid things.' Beau included. Especially Beau.

She looked at him with tears in her eyes, and he pulled her into another hug, this time for her sake. Mostly.

Julie was worrying her bottom lip, phone in hand. 'So... do we call the police?'

Beau shrugged, reluctantly letting go of Céline. She stayed tantalisingly close to him, so he left his hand on the small of her back. 'Was there anything of value in that box?'

'That's the thing. There was only my key collection and a few decorative bits of pewter. A small dish, a lamp base... Ordinarily, I wouldn't hesitate telling the police about a mugging, but... it's you.'

That made him smile in spite of himself. Julie trusted him, which might be naive, but she wasn't stupid. 'Oh, don't worry, my father will hear about this. But we need to inform the police too. If these guys knew who I was, they wouldn't have attacked me, which means the next time they do it, it'll happen to someone who's actually shocked. I think I can give a pretty good description of them.' Complete with names and addresses. But tempting though that was, it would give away the game.

Julie sighed. 'All right. Céline and I will finish packing. You sit in there and switch on the *clima*. We'll report this and then go to Jeanette's for lunch.'

Beau objected that he could help, but Julie wouldn't hear of it and marched him to the van's cabin. With nothing better to do, Beau couldn't help but return to Franck and his reasons for having Beau mugged. *It's you...* Julie had touched on something there that she herself had not even realised. Beau was sure to tell his father that Franck had had him attacked. Again.

When Franck was released from prison, Beau had been shot at. Luckily, only his motorcycle helmet had sustained any damage, but Beau's father had been furious. His mother had let slip that she'd never seen him so angry. Beau had no illusions that this was for Beau's sake rather than because someone had had the audacity to threaten the great Patrick Fouquet's inner circle. All Beau had ever heard about it afterwards was a note saying 'Taken care of'.

He'd tried to find out more, of course. Was he really to take orders from a man who'd had him shot at? But other than vague rumours that Patrick and Franck had fallen out, it was obvious that, apart from being Patrick's son, Beau didn't really count in the family hierarchy. Nothing seemed to have changed after the shooting. Beau continued to live with Julie, looking out for any clues that she had more knowledge about Franck's key than she appeared to have, but not knowing if he was supposed to pick a side, or what the side he was on was telling him to do.

He'd be crazy to do the bidding of a man who wanted him out of the picture. On the other hand, his father hadn't given him any other orders. Hadn't even replied to his messages. Not then, and he wouldn't now after he'd been hit over the head and relieved of a box of worthless junk. Would anything change? Did being Patrick Fouquet's son actually count for anything, or were other family members more important?

He huffed to himself. Of that last thing he was certain. *She* would know. But Beau hadn't talked to her in years...

4
Everything looks amazing!

Though there wasn't technically anything wrong with the *salade Lyonnaise* in front of me, I had been pushing it around my plate for over a minute now. After we'd spoken to a friendly police officer who said they would do everything they could to retrieve the stolen goods but not to have high hopes, we'd retreated to Saint-Maurice to have lunch at the hotel I co-owned with Jeanette Ta. Jeanette's cook, Théo, was an absolute master in the kitchen and could infuse even a simple salad with magic.

Today's salad, however, was anything but magic. For the first time since records began, Théo had called in sick. His sous-chef was perfectly adequate, so I was starting to suspect my lack of enjoyment had more to do with the circumstances than with the actual food. First that strange attack on Thibault for a box of worthless items, and now a business partner who didn't seem to know up from down without her trusty cook.

I had known from the start that Théo's food would be a major draw, and had accordingly offered him a handsome contract. Jeanette, however, seemed only now to realise that she had quietly depended on him for years. Ordinarily, there was nothing Jeanette couldn't handle when it came to the hotel. It had always been her dream to open and run it, but knowing Théo wasn't there in the kitchen for mental support and to bring her food when she'd forgotten to eat again made her dazed and scatterbrained.

I couldn't take it any more. I got up and strode up to the reception desk where Jeanette stood staring into space. 'Go. I'll take care of things here for a bit. Go see how he is and if you can do anything for him. You're no good the way you are now, anyway.'

Surprise, confusion, resistance, and then relief followed each other on Jeanette's face. She finally smiled with a kind of hiccup. 'Thanks, Juju.' Without even changing out of her uniform, she hurried out the door to check on her chef.

Immediately, several members of staff came to me to ask questions they'd been afraid to pose to Jeanette today. They kept me busy for at least fifteen minutes, by which time I was pining for my salad, magic or not. The most pressing matters out of the way, I appointed Jeanette's second in command the boss for the day and abandoned the desk to rejoin Céline and Beau, who both had their eyes glued to their phone screens.

For them, when they were together, this was not normal, and I felt my eyebrows lower. 'Beau? Are you all right?' He wasn't usually the one most affected by a setback. On the contrary, his positive attitude had helped me through many sad moments the last few months, most of them to do with his family.

He looked up and gave me an odd, intense look. I'd only seen this look once before, in the very first days he'd come to live with me, and it made me shiver. Back then, the feeling that there was something he wasn't telling me was natural. He'd shown up out of nowhere after years of no contact, so why would he bare his soul the minute he saw me? In the months that followed, I'd seen more and more of the Beau I knew as a teenager, the friend he used to be, but that nagging feeling remained. In fact, it had become a certainty. I knew there were probably plenty of things he wasn't telling me, but I'd convinced myself it was for my own good and that I didn't want to know. This look, though...

I swallowed after he looked away. Ignoring the niggling doubt about him suddenly seemed like the worst idea. What had started as an impression was now palpable and scary. Had I been a fool to trust him? Or was I a fool now to throw away months of building trust on one frightening moment?

Perhaps it was just me. Beau had been attacked. Of course he wouldn't be his usual self. He couldn't help his family connection. He'd said himself that he'd escaped. But had he? Before someone had shot at him, we'd had a falling out, and he'd gone straight back to his family. On the other hand, someone *had* shot at him.

That thought calmed me, oddly. If he was still part of that world, they wouldn't shoot him. Therefore, I should probably trust him. At least enough to go on as usual and wait for him to tell me what was going on. If anything was going on.

I closed my eyes for a moment to let my instincts get with the program that we were now trusting Beau again and tried to think of something else. That wasn't too difficult. Léon's face popped up in my mind as it usually did. My wonderful boyfriend, an economics professor whose current job was in the US, was coming back in three days. I would probably only have him for a month or so before he'd have to start another contract, but I was determined to make the most of our time together. My calendar was cleared, even though it was the busiest time of year for me. Sometimes, you have to give up something for the person you love. And I did love him so!

The night before, our daily conversation had been wonderfully mundane. He was excited to come back to France but was also complaining about its bureaucracy. How many forms he'd had to fill in just to get his *carte vitale*, his health insurance, back up and running. And all of them sent via snail mail, which was sluggish snail mail when it had to be sent abroad. But he'd said it was all worth it if he could be with me again. Corny, but so nice to hear.

But I couldn't yet devote all my time to Léon. I had a party to prepare for. I cast another hesitant glance at Beau, who'd gone back to his phone screen, then pushed my plate away for good, together with my doubts about him.

'I think I should go and lay out the refreshments. Are you up to it?'

Beau looked up from his phone, all innocence and smiles now. 'Of course, no problem.' Realising he was laying it on too thickly, he reached for the bump on his head. 'I'll let you know if I need to lie down.' He gave me that wink that worked on everyone but me and Céline, which only convinced me more that he wasn't fully there. Distracted, at the very least. Untrustworthy, if I believed my stubborn instinct. But my instinct had been wrong before.

An hour later, the balloons were floating, the raspberries were frozen, Céline had brought over a truckload of macarons, the air conditioning was on, and Beau was humming the tune of the Sugar Plum Fairy, which turned into the *Mission Impossible* theme along the way. I'd checked my mistress list several times over, but all was as it should be. Apart from the fact that this was a marketing tactic I hadn't tried before, everything was so ordinary that the ordinariness itself almost scared me. Somehow, it felt like the attack on Beau was supposed to usher in something even more dangerous, but everything went along as it was supposed to.

As expected, I'd had a message from my elderly client that she and her friends were not coming because of the *canicule*, the heatwave, so I was happy I'd already partially filled their space with Capucine, even though we'd only met that morning. If I was lucky, she'd even bring her own friend. Besides her, I had twelve other guests coming. Two of them, Marie and Nienke, were friends from the village. One, Sandrine Lardy, also lived in Saint-Maurice but I wouldn't count her among my friends. She had married a wealthy businessman and now considered herself above mere mortals. But if she was going to bring me more business in the form of two wealthy friends, who was I to say no to that? In addition to my six unknowns, the three other guests were lovely former clients I couldn't wait to see again.

As arranged, Marie and Nienke were the first to arrive. I'd agreed to them coming early in case Beau and I needed some last-minute help setting up. I'd left the glass front door to my studio open so my guests could come straight in. The air conditioning would counter the heat coming in from outside. Though I felt a bit guilty about the waste of energy, I felt

I'd make it up by not using my studio lights over the coming month when Léon was here.

'*Coucou!* Oh, everything looks amazing!' Nienke's eyes sparkled behind her colourful glasses.

'Is there anything we can do?' Marie asked while giving Beau a hug.

'I think Beau and I pretty much have it covered. How's your head?' I had been so busy with the party preparations that I hadn't even asked him before.

'Oh no! Did you hurt your head? What happened?' Nienke, used to caring for a host of grandchildren constantly falling over, was already reaching for Beau's head, but he stepped back with a grin.

'I got hit over the head but I'm all right.' He rapped his skull with his knuckles. 'Thick skin.'

Marie's eyes widened. 'Hit? Where? When?'

'We were at a *brocante* this morning, and someone hit me and ran off with one of the boxes.'

Marie's horrified look contrasted with Nienke's resigned face. 'I knew it. I could feel evil approaching this morning, as soon as I woke up. I told Marie about it just now as we came up to the door.' Marie nodded. 'I felt it even stronger then, but it must have been because of what happened to you. When I saw all the lovely decorations, the feeling simply disappeared.'

Ordinarily, I didn't pay much attention to Nienke's feelings. This time, though, her words reminded me of my earlier uneasiness. I thought I'd shaken it off, especially after Beau and I had spent the last hour working together as the companionable team we'd grown into, but it turned out my doubt wasn't buried very deeply.

Had the moment come? The moment I'd been expecting but had delayed for ten months? The moment it would be better for my mental and perhaps also physical health to kick Thibault out? If not from my life, then at least from my house. I'd gone back and forth on this ever since he'd shown up, but there was never enough demonstrable reason for me to go through with it. And he'd been the friend I needed on more than one occasion.

I knew he'd have to go at some point. Was my brain just trying to make that break more bearable by blaming him? Or was something bad really about to happen, and distancing myself from Beau would be the only way to prevent it?

Marie and Nienke had already left her statement behind and were cooing over the food and the decorations. Whatever decision I made, it would have to wait till after the party. If nothing else, I needed Beau today to help keep everyone entertained. And chances were, after the party, I'd have forgotten all about my current edginess. It was probably just pre-party jitters.

A weight lifted off my shoulders. See! That was it! I was just nervous about the party. Good. With that established, my smile turned genuine, and I almost skipped to the door to welcome in my first guests.

'Chantelle! So good to see you. Come in, it's nice and cool in here.'

The bubbly woman introduced me to her friend Lela and said she wouldn't hug me this time, as it was far too hot. I couldn't agree more, so we stuck to air kisses. Chantelle had cut off all her blonde hair and was now rocking a short Afro with a shaved flower over one ear. Though she was a recent addition to my client list, she wore her heart on her sleeve, so I knew this style suited her perfectly. Lela was a far quieter sort, with a sweet smile and happy eyes. She was shorter than Chantelle and had a slender face and figure, so next to the presence that was Chantelle, she almost disappeared, but she obviously adored her friend.

Chantelle's first words as she sailed into the studio were directed at Beau. 'Hiya, Blondie. Broken the law lately?'

'I make it a point not to,' he replied rather coolly.

I grinned. Most clients came to my studio a total of three times: once for an initial consultation, once for the shoot, and once for the reveal. But Chantelle was no regular client. She was a carpenter and had built me a ramp for a shoot with a client in a wheelchair. As part of her payment, she'd bargained for a cheap shoot, during which we'd struck up a friendship. She'd come over a few more times, as she was interested in the professional side of my business, and I was only too happy to explain.

And that was probably why Beau wasn't too happy with her. She'd made it clear she'd be interested in an apprenticeship. An *official* apprenticeship. Not just showing up and telling me I needed his help, like someone else had done. Chantelle, of course, knew nothing about how Beau had come to be my assistant, but he certainly saw the difference.

Though I'd been a bit overwhelmed at the time he appeared, Beau had turned into an excellent assistant, and what was more, he'd shown me I did need one. I didn't wonder any longer how he'd come to me, but I'd always known he wouldn't be here forever. He'd learned a lot over the past few months – about composition, working with clients, the workings of different cameras, and post-production – but while his pictures were technically fine, they lacked the vivacity of his drawings. He could be a great artist, but not as a photographer.

Secretly, I was excited to see what fresh influences a new assistant could bring me, but I would never send Beau away for that reason alone. He proved his worth yet again a few minutes later, when I welcomed Agathe, one of my previous clients, and her friend into the studio.

'That's the one I was telling you about!' Agathe called out to her friend, unashamedly pointing at Beau. 'He called me his sheep. Julie was mortified, but I just couldn't stop laughing.'

'Yes, you would appreciate that kind of cheek,' her friend answered. They'd hardly said more than *bonjour* to me, but were already crowding Beau, Agathe babbling about her children, the friend more interested in Beau himself. Beau, however, was unfazed. He smiled, wiggled his eyebrows, flexed his muscles in seemingly unintentional ways, and generally made a spectacle of himself.

I caught an amused look from Chantelle, who was parading around the studio as if she owned it, a glass of champagne in her hand. 'I hope you don't expect all your assistants to make such fools of themselves.'

I had made her no promises, though I'd kept my options open. The way she'd taken my 'maybe' as a 'later' almost made me look forward to working with her. Ten months ago, I would have been far too intimidated by her confidence, but now, and partly thanks to Beau, I had enough confidence in my own capabilities to appreciate self-confidence in others without considering it arrogance.

'No, I only expect it of him.' I folded my arms and shook my head at his shenanigans. I'd entrusted him with one of my cameras, hoping he'd capture the elegant liveliness I was hoping to convey with this party, so I could use the pictures as marketing material. All he was doing with it was showing off.

The next client to arrive was Yolande, the lady for whom Chantelle had built me the ramp. The two friends she brought were as chic and graceful as she was. I introduced them to Capucine, who came in quietly with a friend right after the others. Though elegance alone is not something to form a connection over, it was all I could think of to make Capucine feel at home before I had to turn all my attention to Sandrine Lardy, who sailed into the studio, arms wide.

'Hello, *mes belles*! Ah, aren't you all just gorgeous!'

Had she been at the champagne before she came here? But no, she only drank cucumber water, if I remembered correctly. When she came for her shoot, she'd acted as though her patronage of 'a local business' was what would save me from certain doom. Now, she greeted everyone like old friends, though most, if not all of them, had to be complete strangers to her. The friends she brought, both lanky salon-blondes like Sandrine with disinterested demeanours, could only be distinguished by their mouths, as one had unnaturally pouty lips. Both grabbed a glass of champagne without even acknowledging me, after which one turned a bored eye to the framed pictures of my clients I had on one wall, while the other was staring at Marie's left arm, which stopped at her elbow.

Fortunately, Marie was chatting to Chantelle and didn't notice the rude attention, but I couldn't take it any longer.

'So, how did you like Sandrine's pictures?' I asked the staring blonde.

Lazily, she turned her gaze to me with pupils almost as large as her irises. 'Pictures?'

I forced my mouth into a smile. 'Never mind. Try the macarons, they're delicious.'

Lips had wandered into the dressing room and was wrinkling her nose at the vintage style dresses, plucking at the fabric with her thumb and forefinger. I hesitated on the threshold, then decided she wasn't worth my time and turned back to the guests I did like. Fourteen people in all, six of which had already been clients. Though I would have preferred to join my guests for socialising, this was supposed to be a business opportunity. Now, who to talk to first?

The blondes I immediately discounted. Chantelle's friend was too sweet to go for my saucy photos. Agathe's friend was a maybe, but my best option was the group of refined ladies around Yolande and Capucine. I straightened my back, took a deep breath, and froze.

'Hello?'

That knock. That voice. Icy water trickled down my back and into my veins. Not him. Not now.

5

I was not alone

Thibault was next to me in an instant. I was vaguely aware of my guests staring at me and trying to get a peek at the man by the door, but I couldn't move.

'Stay here. I'll go,' Beau said.

With a jerk of his head, he signalled Marie and Nienke, who hurried over to put their arms around me, but the cold in my heart remained. Sandrine's unsubtle whispering had my shoulders crawl up around my ears, but then I suddenly got an elbow in my ribs. As I unclenched with surprise, someone jerked my shoulders back. I looked up into the furious face of Nienke.

Kind, gentle Nienke was glaring at me. 'If that's who I think it is, don't you dare cower,' she hissed.

I blinked. Somehow, the ice had shattered. I was not alone. Slowly, I swelled back into the shoulders Nienke was still holding. Was I a cowering weakling? No! I was a strong woman. I did not need men. And that man at the door had no power over me!

I looked Nienke in the eye. Smiling was out of the question, but I put my hand over hers and she let go, satisfied. Then I went to join Beau, trying to ignore the heated whispering behind me.

As I approached the door, the heat outside won over the air-conditioned coolness in my studio. Before I'd even reached my unwanted visitor, I could already feel sweat breaking out. He looked... exactly the same. Years in prison had not changed Franck Fouquet, except maybe for the little beard he'd grown, but to me, it didn't make him any more or less attractive, nor repulsive. He was just... Franck. The lowest of the low, yes, but nothing to do with me. As I let this feeling of freedom course through my body, it was all I could do not to dance for joy.

Four years I had lived in fear of seeing him again, and now that I did, it was the best thing that could have happened. The only thing that could have truly convinced me I was free of him. Free of the fear of him. I could have kissed... not him. Beau, maybe, but judging from Beau's face, this was not the time. His dark look brought me back to the moment. If I was free of Franck, why was he here?

'Julie.' That beautiful, soft baritone that had once bowled me over now did nothing to me. His tone was friendly and his expression full of care and regret, but I knew not to trust anything about that man. 'Dear, dear Julie.' He paused for effect, then sighed. 'I'm sorry.' Another pause. Both Beau and

I waited with unbelieving patience. 'I'm so, so sorry. You have to believe me. Prison has changed me.'

At this, Beau huffed. 'Spare us. What do you want.' It sounded more like a threat than a question. Beau's hands were on his hips. He seemed calm, but I could see an artery in his neck pulsing quickly.

'I know. I know. I shouldn't have come. I wouldn't have, only... I need help.' A flicker of genuine distress shot through Franck's eyes.

If it were anyone else, seeing them in distress would have prompted me to try and help. This morning, it would have delighted me to see something bad happen to Franck, but now, seeing him in distress was simply an observation. I felt nothing, good or bad. 'What could you possibly need my help with?'

Relief loosened his stance. 'Thank you, for at least listening to me.'

'Be quick, I have more important things to do.' Also, the heat was unbearable at this time of day, as the sun shone directly on this side of the house and it was difficult to even look at Franck. If he'd been any taller, I would have been looking directly into the sun, but I preferred my men on the shorter side.

'*Bien sur.* Thing is, I heard you've become kind of a sleuth. You may be aware that one of Patrick's men has gone missing?'

I gave a short nod. There had been a mutiny in the organisation led by Beau's father. Beau had played a starring role in resolving the situation, but the leader of the rebels had disappeared afterwards.

'*Eh ben...* The police think he's dead. They think I killed him. They're building a case against me, and I didn't know who else to turn to.'

I reached over to Beau and guided him inside. As I turned to follow him, I said over my shoulder, 'I don't do missing persons.' And then I shut the door in his face.

One. Two. Three. Still with my hand on the opaque glass door, I watched Franck's feet disappear. Then I collapsed.

Beau was just in time to catch me, and he hugged me tight, despite the weather. 'That. Was. Awesome! When did you become such a bad—'

'What happened?' Marie and Nienke came hurrying into the hallway.

'She only showed Franck who's boss.' Beau was elated, though he was still supporting me. His excitement finally made me smile, and I made a strong effort to get back on my feet.

'I couldn't have done it without you,' I said softly. I meant it, but my stomach clenched. What if Beau hadn't been here? What if Franck came back one day after Beau left? I tried not to think about that, but my stomach was still churning.

Thibault waved a hand and shook his head, laughing. 'Oh yes, you could. I mean, maybe you would have been on the floor now, but that's just because it's the first time. Next time you see him, you'll have practice and you can put him in his place even better. Here.' He handed me a glass of champagne and clinked it with one of his own. 'A toast!' he called out to everyone in the studio. 'To strong women, and the people lucky enough to be around them!'

Everyone but the vacant blonde cheered. The champagne may have played a part in it, but his words warmed me all the way through, even though I was standing right underneath the air conditioning unit. Slowly, my heart rate returned to normal, and some of Beau's euphoria seeped through. I had faced Franck and come out on top! If none of those women booked a session, today would still be a success. I *was* a strong woman. And Franck had nothing to do with that, one way or another.

Beau had switched on the music, which woke up even the blondes. While everyone started dancing, I took up the camera Beau had left on a table when Franck arrived. Somehow, I felt even stronger with the heavy, black machine in my hand. I took a few snapshots, trying to capture as many happy faces as I could, but then Yolande waved me over.

'Are you all right? What happened back there?'

With sudden embarrassment, I chewed my bottom lip, then pulled up a chair and sat next to the classy lady in the wheelchair. 'I'm sorry you had to witness that. It's hardly party material.'

'Your friends said something about a criminal ex-husband?'

Keeping my eyes on my champagne glass, I nodded. 'He threatened to kill me when he went to jail. This was the first time I've seen him since he came out.'

'But he obviously hasn't killed you.'

That made me laugh. 'No. He...' Hmm. Now that I thought about it, his request was highly remarkable. 'He said he needed my help.'

Yolande narrowed her dark eyes but didn't say anything.

I frowned. I'd been so relieved to have survived my run-in that I hadn't questioned Franck's motives for being there in the first place.

Yolande's gentle hand on my arm made me jump. 'Now is not the time to worry about that.' She smiled. 'I'd love another glass of champagne. Would you mind?'

Though she was perfectly capable of getting it herself, I was grateful that she pushed me to occupy myself with other things. Franck wasn't worth any time I could instead spend enjoying my own party. I delivered the champagne and held up my camera again, only Beau reached over my head from behind and took it from me.

'That was my job for the day, remember? You were going to talk to potential clients. Now smile.'

I made a face, which Beau captured, though I doubted he could have adjusted the focus quickly enough.

'Julie?'

Of course my weird face had been witnessed by one of Yolande's refined friends. But after the humiliation of having to deal with my personal past in the middle of a party for strangers, I hardly cared any more.

'I'm Océane, I came with Yolande?' The brunette with wide, watery blue eyes gave me a wide smile. 'I was already impressed when she showed me the photos you'd done of her, but I've been looking around and I'm convinced. Can I make a booking right now?'

I was happy to confirm and led the way to my office.

'Ooh, me too!' Agathe's friend hurried after us, followed by Capucine.

This was going well! I booked them all in for initial consultations and gave Capucine, who was the last to remain, a satisfied smile. 'I hope you've been enjoying yourself, despite the earlier... glitch.'

She waved my concern away. 'It was nothing to us, *chérie.* I'm glad you were all right. Who was that man? If you don't mind me asking.'

I shook my head. 'Franck Fouquet. My ex-husband.'

'Ah.' She gave a small smile. 'I've heard they can be the worst.' Then her gaze turned thoughtful. 'Franck Fouquet. The name seems familiar. I know I haven't heard it in a long time, but there's something...'

I raised my eyebrows. What possible connection could someone as exquisite as Capucine have with Franck? But as I was already at my computer, I typed his name into Google and turned the screen towards Capucine to show her his picture. The effect was astonishing.

'Him!' Capucine cried, standing up so quickly that her chair toppled backwards and crashed to the floor. She cast me a wild look that was so out of character it shook my already strained nerves to the point I felt my lip wobble.

'I *hate* him!' Her voice came out raspy, but that seemed to bring her to her senses. She brought her fingers to her lips, then to the silk shawl around her neck. 'Oh, excuse me. I'm terribly sorry. The shock, you see... That man tried to swindle me. It was years ago, but the trouble I had...' She took a deep breath. 'Again, I'm sorry. I can see why he had such an impact on you. All I can say is...' She straightened her back. 'I'm glad you showed him who's boss.'

Though trembling slightly, she now stood ramrod straight, her knuckles white on her purse. Seeing my own feelings about Franck played out like that by someone I hardly knew felt surreal. Strangely though, it also felt liberating. As though seeing my feelings mirrored in someone else took them out of me. Still shaky myself, I stood as well, not knowing what to say but making sure my chin was in the air.

Another uncharacteristic thing happened. Capucine grinned. 'Yes. I like you. I'm looking forward to my shoot. And now I should go find my friend.'

She marched out of my office, and I deflated into my chair. What just happened? I held up my hand and saw it still shaking rather more than I wanted it to. What a day. I was ready for this party to be over, but we were only an hour in. After another few deep breaths, I rose and left my office but hovered at the door to observe my party without me there.

Thibault had already recovered from seeing Franck at my door. He was surrounded by the new ladies and probably calling them all kinds of animal names. How he managed to make that endearing... Still, I was used to girls sucking in their bellies when he came near. Apparently, he had a similar effect on women over forty. Though I still maintained my business would survive just fine without him. With a smile, I joined his group of admirers.

Océane, the blue-eyed brunette who had kicked off the bookings, moistened her lips. 'Tell me, does he model for you?'

Beau smirked. Océane had probably meant to ask that at a more discreet tone than the champagne had elicited.

'No, he's just here for decoration,' I answered equally loudly.

Beau's jaw dropped in mock indignation. 'I resent that!'

I was about to answer with another quip, but Capucine tapped me on the shoulder.

'Have you seen my friend Delphine? I can't find her any-where.'

6

The police are on their way

I looked around the room, supposedly to check if I could spot Delphine where Capucine hadn't searched, but really trying to remember what she looked like. Ordinarily, it was my job to study people's faces, but today had been one shock after another, and with all these new people in my studio, I had to really make an effort to recall Delphine's physiognomy.

Let's see, she'd come in with Capucine right after Yolande and her friends. Ah, yes, that was it. She'd been stylishly dressed, blending in with the other four women in that little group. But what had made her stand out slightly was that she was not blessed in the looks department, with the body of a silver birch and the face of a daffodil. Still, I could make it work with the right pose and the right lighting. And the magic of my make-up artist, of course.

But where was she? With Capucine in my wake, I searched the dressing room, then the kitchenette, checked my office again, and even went upstairs to Beau's floor, but Delphine was nowhere to be found. Returning to the party, I called out over the music, 'Has anyone seen Delphine?'

The chatter stopped for a moment so people could smile and shrug at me but then swelled again. Nienke frowned in alarm, but I purposely looked away. I couldn't be dealing with one of her feelings right now.

Instead, my gaze fell, inadvertently but directly, on the stoned blonde, whose eyes widened as if she'd been called out. 'I haven't seen her since she went out.'

'Out? Out where?' Why would anyone willingly go out into that heat when there was literally a cool party going on inside?

She gestured to the door leading to the patio. I glanced at Capucine, who shrugged.

'Perhaps she thought that was the way to the ladies' room?'

Instead of answering, I opened the door and forced myself into the oven outside. This was the shady side of the house, but the sun was still bright enough to blind me for a second or two. I closed the door behind me to keep the cool in and veered towards the left, where a roofed section of wall between my studio and the house provided just a little bit more shelter from the heat.

I was on my way towards the house, though I was pretty sure I'd locked that door, when my eyes adjusted to the light and I skidded to a halt. For two long seconds, my brain refused to comprehend what I saw. Then, it went into overdrive, and I blacked out.

I awoke on the white leather couch in my studio with Thibault slapping my cheek. My first instinct was to swat him away, but then reality hit me and I shot up straight.

'Delphine! She...' I retched, remembering her limp body lying in a pool of blood.

'We know,' Beau said in a low voice, gently pushing me back down onto the pillow. 'The police are on their way.'

'Jacqueline...' I started, but stopped even before Beau interrupted.

'She quit, remember? She's moving to America with Ken. I don't know who they're going to send, but I hope they're better at dealing with Capucine than Marie and Nienke are.'

Only then did I register the loud wailing coming from the dressing room. I lifted my head again to glance around my studio, where the shiny party decorations formed a garish contrast to the gloomy faces around me.

I sat up, ignoring Beau's concern. 'Who came out to find me?'

'Chantelle thought it was strange you didn't return, so she looked out. She couldn't see exactly what was going on, but enough to keep Capucine from going after her friend and to warn me. I brought you in and called the police.'

'Did you see…' I trailed off but circled my temple with my finger.

He nodded. 'I expect the police will want to know if you own a pair of black Louboutins.'

I retched again, wishing I hadn't had that champagne before. 'Not any more. Those are gone.' I'd eyed the red-soled beauties for months, but on the budget I'd had during my marriage, they were an unattainable dream. When my photography business took off, they were the first frivolous purchase I splurged on. But now… 'Even if they give them back to me… after… I don't want them any more.' I put my hand on his arm and looked him in the eye. 'Are you okay?'

He seemed a little surprised that I asked but didn't immediately answer. He always made out to be the stolid one, the person I could count on when things became a little too much for a strong woman to handle. But even with his background and slightly world-wise attitude, I doubted he'd seen the result of someone taking a stiletto heel to the temple before.

When he kept silent, I leaned over and hugged him tightly. He held me close for longer than usual, then whispered, 'I'll be all right. You?'

I let go but stayed close to him and produced a quivering smile, flexing my biceps to show him I was a strong woman. He smiled too, gave me another quick hug, then took a deep breath to go meet the police. I made sure to be up and beside him by the time they entered the studio. This wasn't his responsibility. *I* wasn't his responsibility.

The men strolling into my domain – one tall, black, and older; one young and red-faced – were no strangers to me. I'd met both Étienne Chagrin and Joseph Rouletabille on separate occasions in my dealings with the police on earlier cases. But they had never come to *my* house for a murder that *I* was involved in.

'You're Jacqueline Gavel's friend, aren't you?' was Chagrin's greeting. 'Did you find the body?'

I swallowed, then nodded.

'And this is your... establishment?' he asked while judging one of my framed photographs.

'It is.' I was happy to hear the defiance in my own shaky voice.

'And the... er... victim is through here?' he added when I pointed at the door. 'All right. Rouletabille, take their statements while I let the *techniciens* in.'

The round face of the brigadier-chef smiled at us when he invited us to sit. I was all too happy to talk to him instead of

Chagrin, as he seemed to possess more intelligence and less arrogance than his colleague.

'What happened to Dupin?' I asked after his former partner as an ice breaker.

Rouletabille tapped his tablet. 'He took the place of Capitaine Gavel.'

So he'd finally got that promotion to Jacqueline's rank. The sleazy way. It was Christophe A. Dupin who'd had my friend taken off her case before she decided to quit. Though Rouletabille was better off without him, I doubted Chagrin would be much of an improvement. 'How do you like your new partner?'

Ignoring the question, Rouletabille asked his own. 'In your own words, can you tell me what happened?'

For the second time that day, I had to relate the events of the past few hours. Rouletabille listened attentively, but there wasn't all that much to tell. At least Capucine had stopped crying so I could focus on my story. I hadn't seen Delphine since before Franck showed up. After that, I'd been preoccupied with getting over the encounter and then signing people up for shoots. When that was done, Capucine had come to me almost immediately, and I'd made my horrible discovery.

'Do you know of anyone who might have wanted to harm her?'

I shrugged and held up my palms. 'I'd only just met her. I hadn't even said more than *bonjour et bienvenue*. You'll have to ask Capucine about the rest.'

'And how do you know Capucine?'

'I met her at a *vide-grenier* this morning.'

'And where is she?'

I got up and led him to the dressing room, where Capucine was still sniffing into a mountain of tissues, but at least she'd gone quiet. I was about to join Nienke and Marie, giving Capucine privacy with the police, but she held out her hand.

'Can you stay, please, Julie? If you're up to it?'

I hesitated. I could really do with a glass of water and some peace and quiet, but here was a person who'd just lost a friend and needed my help.

'Of course, if the chef allows.'

Rouletabille nodded and I sat in one of the chairs Marie and Nienke had vacated.

'I'm sorry for your loss,' he began.

Capucine nodded.

'Can you tell me your name?'

'Capucine Jamin,' she whispered.

'And how long had you known Delphine...?'

'Montpertuis. About a year or two. We met at a flower arranging workshop and were immediate friends. I know who killed her.'

I recoiled in my chair. Rouletabille also seemed perplexed at her sudden declaration, but Capucine was suddenly very calm and collected.

'It was *her* ex-husband, Franck Fouquet.' She pointed to me.

Rouletabille looked at me, and I looked at him.

'What would be his reason for killing your friend?' he asked Capucine.

She made an impatient gesture. 'I don't know. You'll have to ask him. But he was here and he's a criminal. Who else would want to kill Delphine?'

'That's what we're here to find out.' Rouletabille remained much calmer than I was. Franck *had* been here. Everything in me wanted to believe Capucine and lock him away for good, but if I gave myself half a second to think about her accusation, it made no sense at all. Did Franck even know Delphine? And how could he have known she'd be here when I hadn't even known myself before she actually arrived?

Rouletabille had asked if Delphine had any enemies, and Capucine was shaking her head. 'No. I'm telling you, it was him.'

The tiniest pursing of his lips gave away Rouletabille's resignation on the subject, but I doubted Capucine would have noticed that. He changed tactics and asked how they both came to be at the party.

'Oh. Well. In this kind of heat, nobody makes any plans, do they? So when I met Julie this morning, and she asked if I wanted to come to her party, I said I would love to. And Delphine is always the first person I think to ask. She didn't have any plans either, so we came together.'

'Was she enjoying the party?'

She shrugged. 'As far as I know.'

'And when did you last see her?'

She cast her eyes down and shifted in her chair. I gently squeezed her hand to show her my support.

'I should have paid more attention to her, but I was talking to this lady in a wheelchair who seemed like a nice person. Delphine asked me where the toilet was, which, of course, I didn't know, so I just... waved her away. Or something. I don't remember.' Her lower lip wobbled and she burst into another wail. 'I don't even remember my last moments with her!' Burying her face in tissues, she cried loudly, making the young brigadier-chef decidedly uncomfortable.

'Perhaps you should go and talk to some of the others first, so they can leave if they want?' I suggested.

With a relieved smile, he nodded and said he'd be back. But now I was stuck by myself with a miserable woman and nothing positive to say to her. My offer of a glass of water was turned down, so there was nothing left for me to do but sit there and pat her hand.

To keep my brain from showing me the horrific image of Delphine lying on my patio, I forced my thoughts to be logical. Someone had come to my house to take my shoe – I assumed it was my shoe though I hadn't checked whether mine were still there – and use it to violently kill someone who'd only decided to be here a few hours in advance.

On the one hand, the choice of victim almost had to have been made at random. On the other, using something of mine as a weapon couldn't be anything but premeditated. Then again, who picks a shoe as a weapon? But why would they steal my shoe in the first place, if killing was what they set out to do? Or why would they kill anyone, if all they wanted was to steal my shoes?

Perhaps it depended on who the someone was. As much as I tried to be impartial, Capucine's accusation did seem the most attractive one. Franck had been here right around the time the murder had taken place. My guests had all been inside, where it was cool, and who else would have had – or forced – access to my shoes... I mean, my house?

Had the door in my courtyard wall been locked? Usually, it was. But since the killer had stolen my shoes, it was obvious they'd come through from my house, and they would have retreated through there as well, perhaps even leaving a trail through my living room, judging from the messy scene in the courtyard...

I retched again, making Capucine look up.

'I'm so sorry,' I squeaked.

'No, I'm sorry.' The genuine regret in her voice calmed my stomach. 'I never thought about you. Perhaps I can get you some water?'

'Let's get some together,' I decided. 'If you're ready?'

Capucine dumped her hoard of tissues in the waste paper basket and stood up straight. 'As I'll ever be.'

I plucked a few more tissues from the dressing table as we exited, just in case, and rounded the corner to the little kitchen at the front of the studio, trying not to look at the front door and imagine Franck's feet there. I'd overcome my first meeting with him only to fall back into fear almost immediately after.

Only... the fear was different this time. If it *had* been him, he could have simply waited for another occasion to walk in and kill me. Delphine looked nothing like me, so he couldn't have mistaken her for me. Did that mean he didn't intend to kill me? But if the shoe was meant to implicate me in someone else's murder, his methods had got far more sloppy than they used to be. He was always so very meticulous in everything he did. Then again, as far as I knew, he'd never killed anyone. At least not till now.

As I filled two glasses and handed one to Capucine, I risked a question. 'Did Franck know Delphine?'

Capucine narrowed her eyes at me. '*Non*. I don't think so. I mean, I must have told her at some point about what he did to me, but as far as I know, they moved in very different circles.'

'And he was in prison until four months ago.' I pursed my lips. Franck had never been one to do things randomly. But if he had *not* done this, that left the very unsettling possibility that some madman had found his way into my house to murder the first person they saw with whatever they had to hand. I shivered.

'There you are!' Yolande hovered at the entrance to the little kitchen.

While she hesitated, Capucine moved past me. 'I should go find that police officer.'

With Capucine gone, Yolande rolled into the kitchen. 'Is she all right? Are you all right?'

I nodded, not wanting to speak the lie. 'I'm sorry you had to be part of this.'

'Oh, don't worry about us.' She flashed an easy smile. 'That's actually what I came to tell you. They've realised my friends and I aren't really involved, so we're allowed to leave. I think we'll just... go.'

I nodded again. 'Of course. I wouldn't want to stay either. I hope you can all soon forget this ever happened.'

'And you, Julie. Let me know if there's anything I can do.'

She wheeled herself backwards, ready to leave, but I stopped her.

'Oh, Yolande, there is something. Capucine says her memories of the last moments with her friend are vague because she was talking to you. She's terribly upset about it. Can you remember what happened?'

Yolande's eyebrows dropped in compassion and she put her hand over her heart. 'Of course. I've just told that policeman about it. Capucine had complimented me on my skirt and was interested to know where I'd got it, so when her friend asked if she knew where the littlest room was, she looked around and waved at the door to the courtyard, saying something like "Perhaps through there?" and then she continued our conversation, so I didn't actually pay attention to whether the friend went out or not. She must have done...'

Yolande winced, but her friends had gathered at the door, so she joined them to leave. I let them out into the oppressive mid-afternoon heat and quickly closed the door behind them. The lanky blondes were next to leave, without so much as an acknowledgement of what had happened, but Sandrine enveloped me in an unexpected hug.

'Isn't it awful? Here we are again, in the same building with a dead person. A *murdered* person. I'm glad I was with my friends this time, so nobody can accuse me.'

I wondered if the blondes had really paid that much atten-tion to her. Or, if they did, whether they'd remember. But if it made Sandrine feel better to believe that, I wouldn't burst her bubble.

She paused, biting a manicured nail and glancing at her companions. 'Look, if you... would rather not stay here tonight... I mean, I know you have Beau and everything... What I'm saying is, you're welcome to stay with us. Both of you. We have a few guests staying already, but the house is big enough.'

She was right, there. Only my brother's eighteenth-century mansion could rival her modern villa in size.

'We both know what it's like trying to sleep in a house where someone's been murdered and I'd rather you not go through that again. Please say you'll at least consider it.'

I blinked at her sudden altruism. This human side of her was new to me. 'All right, I'll think about it. Thanks.' Though I'd no intention of taking her up on her offer, having the option to leave lifted my spirits. I could probably stay at the hotel if necessary, but Sandrine's friendly offer warmed me.

The blondes left together with Agathe and her friend, as well as Chantelle and her friend Lela, who looked utterly miserable.

'I'm sorry it didn't turn out the way I'd hoped,' was all I could say.

Chantelle assured me they'd get over it, and she'd be back if I needed her. After that, I was left with just Beau, my two friends, Capucine, and a bunch of police people. I felt for the crime scene investigators, having to wear those overalls in such heat. Perhaps I could offer them some cool drinks. I had plenty left over from my now sad-looking party.

Nienke, Marie, and Thibault were quietly clearing away the decorations, while in the corner, near the fake fireplace, Brigadier-Chef Rouletabille was finishing up his interview with a still sniffling Capucine. I hadn't seen Major Chagrin since he went outside but wasn't keen on seeing more of him.

'Can I offer you a drink, Chef?' I asked when he'd put away his tablet and Capucine was making her way to the door. 'And perhaps your colleagues would like some too? There are fresh bottles in the fridge, if you can't use what's in here.'

His round face shone as he went outside to ask the people working there. Nienke was already pulling bottles from the fridge, while Marie reached for Capucine and asked if she had someone she could stay with.

'Thank you, yes. That policeman has already called them and they're on their way. Oh, don't look like that, Julie. I know none of this is your fault.' She placed a quivering hand on my arm. 'It'll be all right, I promise. I've lost someone dear before. I got over it then and I will again. You try and do that too.'

I wanted to say, 'as soon as they've caught the killer', but then I remembered she was convinced it was Franck, and I didn't want to make her any more upset than she already was.

Marie took Capucine under her wing and made sure she was out of the way before the people in the white suits entered. Though they were not irreverent, they were here simply to do their job, not to hold anyone's hand. I showed them into the kitchenette, but when one of them made a joke about their child loving balloons even though they were thirteen already, my breath hitched. How were there people in my house whose lives were continuing untouched by what had occurred? Did they not understand the gravity of the situation?

But then, to them, this happened regularly. It was their job to photograph and take samples of people who had met an untimely end. They couldn't, and shouldn't, live in a state of eternal gloom. We all need a job, and not everyone can spend their day taking photos of women showing their underwear. Perhaps my job was shocking to them too. Although I doubted it.

I hadn't realised I'd been standing in the middle of the corridor staring at the people in my kitchen until Beau pushed the glass in my hand up to my lips.

'Have a sip. If you're listening in on someone's conversation, try and be a little less conspicuous about it.'

I frowned at him. 'I wasn't—'

'Then perhaps you should.'

7

A symbol of all you've achieved

The two in the kitchen had been discussing the birthday party of one of their children, so Beau couldn't have meant them. But just outside the door to my studio were two others, sipping ice cold water with serious faces. Putting his arm around me as if to comfort me, Beau shuffled me towards the door that had been left open after the departure of Chantelle and Lela, until we were within earshot of the two police investigators.

'No, nothing,' one of them, a woman, was saying. 'Not on any of the doors, inside or out. But none of them were locked.'

'So they had a key.' The other, a man, took a sip.

'Drawing conclusions is not part of my job.'

The sipper frowned. 'You and your rules. If there's no sign of a break-in, there was a key. Right?'

The woman only shrugged and opened her own drink.

Beau, who was still holding my hand in pretend comfort, kept his voice just above a whisper. 'Are you sure you didn't have the house key in that basket?'

I pressed my lips together and narrowed my eyes at him. 'What do you take me for? Besides, how would the thief know which one to take and then come here with it? No, someone must have come here specifically to do this. But who? It makes no sense.'

'I think we both know who.'

For several breaths, I looked him in the eye. 'Unless you know more than I do, he's never killed before.'

'He was here. That whole penitent act, I don't buy it.'

'But why this woman? Capucine said she didn't think Franck had any kind of connection to Delphine. And why the shoe?'

'Because it was yours. Because it's a symbol of all you've achieved without him. In spite of him.'

I didn't want to oppose him, but it sounded far-fetched to me. So far, though, it was the only explanation we had for the unusual choice of weapon, so I changed the subject.

'I think... I don't want to stay in a hotel tonight. Even if it's my own. Too many people with keys. Does that make sense?' He lifted his chin in a silent answer. 'Sandrine has invited us to stay with her tonight, if...?' I left the question unspoken, but he was already nodding.

'Oh yes. As soon as they let us leave, we are out of here.'

Nienke and Marie announced their departure with a wish they could do more. Marie squeezed my arm, saying she was sure I'd have it all figured out before the police even got started. I tried to produce a brave smile, but judging from her pitying reaction, I failed miserably. Capucine left with Chagrin, only sending me a watery smile on the way to the door.

'I'm afraid both the studio and the house are part of the crime scene. You'll have to find somewhere else, at least for the night,' Rouletabille told us.

I glanced at the crime scene investigators still calmly having a drink. 'Have they already been in here?' Though I'd been away in the dressing room and kitchen for a while, I hadn't seen any of them searching for evidence in my studio.

'We did a quick sweep, but as this is a relatively public space and you were having a party, there are likely to be too many unrelated samples to be relevant to the crime. However, we do need to process the scene correctly. We'll let you know when you can return.'

'Can we at least grab a few things for the night?'

He nodded. 'As long as one of us comes along.'

He gave us his card, the card of a professional cleaning company, and the number of the psychologist who worked with them on what he called 'these cases', asked if there was anything else he could do, and left.

'How many of "these cases" do you think he has?' I asked Beau. I didn't like the bitterness in my voice, but I forgave myself when I considered the day I'd had.

'Probably processing Louboutin stiletto heels on a daily basis,' Beau agreed. 'Come on, let's go pack. Do you want me to come with you?'

I paused. My first reaction was 'of course not'. I didn't need him there when I went through my underwear drawer. But then, what if the killer was still in my house? Had those technical people really checked everywhere?

Thibault understood my silence and was out into the courtyard before I'd even moved. I hurried after him and noticed he, too, was keeping his face turned slightly towards the right, away from the porch. Neither of us wanted to be reminded. As much as we'd had to deal with murders in the past year, they had never come this close. I decided to call the therapist who'd worked with me after I left Franck, but first, we needed to get away from here.

One of the white suits had followed us and now let us into the house. Both Beau and I hesitated on the threshold, looking in as though seeing my living room for the first time. But everything was exactly as I'd left it that morning. Nothing had been disturbed, not even the fashion magazine on the couch. The only thing in my house that I hadn't put there were stains of fingerprint powder.

'*Super,*' I muttered. Just what I needed after today: clean-up.

I quickly went upstairs and opened the wardrobe. At a glance from me, Beau came closer, while the white suit kept a watchful eye out from the threshold.

'I always keep the gate locked,' I whispered.

'I know. I use it more than you, since I take my Harley inside. Why?'

Rummaging in my closet so the officer wouldn't suspect, I answered, 'Those people outside said all the doors were unlocked. Inside and out.'

'And?'

I almost growled at his obtuseness. 'The front door and the courtyard door are opened by the same key. The gate key is different.'

His jaw went slack. 'He had both keys.'

I nodded.

'And you still don't believe it was Franck?'

I opened my mouth but could only take a few breaths. Franck wanting to corrupt my private space in the most horrible way possible made complete sense. However, I had been married to this man. Killing an innocent bystander just to get at me, that seemed several leaps too far. Could prison really have changed him that much?

Beau seemed to think so. Maybe he knew more about it than I did and I should listen to him. But Franck had always prided himself on his methodical approach, leaving nothing to chance. He couldn't possibly have known that Delphine would be out there around the time he showed up.

A new thought struck me. 'Do you think Anne-Bonny could have seen something?'

My influencer neighbour was always spying on me, trying to steal my poses, my marketing techniques, and anything else she could get her hands on. Because of that, I hadn't told her about my party, but I wouldn't be surprised if she had noticed people arriving and come to spy on me. Even in a heatwave. She'd probably wear a bikini made of knit spaghetti, or something similarly ridiculous.

Beau shrugged, checking his phone. 'Nothing on social media. Knowing her readiness to get ahead over your back, I think she would have posted about it by now if she knew anything.'

I nodded, resigned. On the one hand, that meant this whole thing might not have the wide negative impact it might have had. On the other, Anne-Bonny might have been a valuable witness.

As I packed a few things and Beau frowned at the size of my suitcase, I couldn't help looking for the Louboutin box in my wardrobe, but though all my other shoe boxes were still there, that particular one was missing.

'Excuse me,' I asked the white suit, 'Did you or one of your colleagues take a box from here?'

The suit nodded, then said with an unexpectedly female voice, 'Naturally. That was evidence.'

'So...' I couldn't form the words to my thought, but the woman helped me out.

'Only one red stiletto heel.'

Perhaps I should have expected it, but the thought of the solitary shoe still shocked me. If someone had meant to steal my expensive shoes, they would have taken the box. Instead, they deliberately took out the one shoe for that most malicious purpose.

I exchanged a glance with Thibault. If I'd doubted it before, it now became painfully obvious that someone, whether that was Franck or not, had meant to take something that specifically belonged to me.

'But it can't have been his intention to murder Delphine with it.'

Beau narrowed his eyes. 'If he went out through the court-yard door, he could potentially have been seen through the window in the studio door. Do you think he meant to stay in the porch area and Delphine surprised him?'

I hesitated. That was a surprisingly plausible explanation. Only... 'What could he possibly want to do there?'

'Wait for you?'

'In a heatwave? With my shoe? I'd have been on my guard and stayed well away from him, unlike Delphine.'

'What else could he have wanted your shoe for?'

'I have no idea!' I thrust one of the other shoe boxes at him. 'Here's another one, see what you can do with it. "Murder someone" wouldn't have been my first suggestion before it actually happened.'

My voice had been climbing in both tone and volume. Beau took the box from me, closed it, and put it back in the wardrobe. 'Let's just go. This isn't helping.'

Fighting my tears, I finished packing and accompanied him back to the studio, leaving the woman in the suit to lock up. While Beau went up with another suit, I turned to the woman and asked if they needed anything more from me. She said no, thanked me for the drinks, and awkwardly wished me a good day. They probably never dealt with the human aftermath of murder. To be fair, I'd only witnessed it from a distance myself up till now. How I wished it could have stayed at a distance.

Beau came down with only a backpack over his shoulder, which I gaped at.

'You don't know how long we'll be staying there. We haven't even called the cleaners yet.'

He shrugged. '*Bof.* So I'll come back for more if I need it.'

This concept was so far beyond my comprehension that I mulled it over in the car all the way to the other side of the village. Sandrine lived just out of view from my house, on the other side of the hill opposite me. There was no mistaking her house, as it was a massive modern villa with sleek, white walls and out-of-context columns. Needless to say, its style wouldn't have attracted me, but its murderlessness was a huge bonus.

I'd let Sandrine know we were on our way, and she came out to welcome us with her usual dramatic flair. Arms wide, eyebrows drooping, she projected at us the moment she came out the front door.

'*Chéris!* I'm so glad you came! Let our humble abode be your refuge for as long as you need it.'

Beau inserted himself in the hug that was coming for me, and Sandrine seemed only too happy to leave it at that. It was a relatively small gesture compared to the care he'd shown me earlier, but it hit me with an unexpected blow of anticipatory nostalgia for the moment he'd be gone from my life. Not every day would include something as big as a murder, but I'd have to brave life's everyday inconveniences without him soon.

Still, I had him now, so I made sure to show my appreciation when he lugged my suitcase out of the car and carried it inside. A bewildered look was all I got for my – perhaps just a tad overstated – gratitude.

Inside the mansion, the walls and fittings were just as angular and stark as the outside. Though not exactly minimalist, the interior held only the necessary furniture. A side table supported a glass dish for keys and that was all for the entire sizeable hallway. There was no coat rack, so I assumed the door by the entrance was a cloakroom. To the right, an archway led to a corridor, while on the left, a double glass door showed a vast sitting room.

'I'll show you to your rooms, and then I'll introduce you,' Sandrine said over her shoulder as she ascended the wide stairs at the back of the hallway. 'Unless you'd rather be alone for a while?'

Surprised by her thoughtfulness, I shook my head, instantly regretting my action. But perhaps, I tried to reason to myself, it was better to keep my mind occupied with meeting new people. My mind was only half convinced, doubting the appeal of anyone Sandrine could introduce me too. Then I scolded myself mentally. I was grateful to her for providing a bit of sanctuary, so I should also be graceful towards her and her guests.

Beau was surprisingly quiet, however, and when she'd shown him his room, he said, 'I think I will stay here for a while, if you don't mind.'

My mouth fell open, but Sandrine only placed a delicate hand on his arm. 'Of course, *mon petit*. Dinner is at eight, but if you're not up to it, I'll have it brought up to you.'

Oh my. Room service. If I'd known that...

'And this is yours.' Sandrine opened the door to another cavernous room in white.

I wheeled my suitcase inside and turned to her with genuine gratitude.

An uncharacteristically awkward smile passed over her face. 'Don't be silly. I'm only too happy to be of help.' Then she collected herself and opened another door. 'En suite through here with an extra-large bathtub. Bath salts, bath tea, bath bombs. Do use them, they're divine. All right, let me introduce you to my guests.'

She left, expecting me to follow. I cast one last, longing glance at the bath tub, then hurried after Sandrine.

'Two of them you've already met. Natalya and Astrid, who came with me to your little party.'

I wondered which of the lanky blondes was Lips, and which Pupils.

'They came with Ronan. Ronan and Sebastian are really here for Emile, but I always treat his friends as mine.'

Wasn't that how all married couples did things? My only experience had been skewed. Franck's friends were either creeps like Cyprien, whom I did not want to be friends with, or they were more like business partners who took no interest in me whatsoever. I should have known what was coming, but before we were married, Franck had given me so much attention that I hadn't picked up on those clues. I had found a replacement for the father I missed so much, and that was it. No brain power involved. I sincerely hoped that was not how Sandrine and Emile's marriage worked.

We entered the ballroom-sized living room, where two men were speaking in English on navy velvet couches positioned perpendicular to each other around a glass coffee table. Both looked up and gave me a friendly smile, but in completely different ways. The round-faced, jolly man was introduced as Ronan Kelly. He had a short, brown beard and hardly ever stopped talking. He asked me in an Irish accent whether I spoke English and, when I said yes, professed to be delighted that he wouldn't have to murder any more French. He then proceeded to ask me all about my life, my business, and my family without ever giving me time to answer. He'd already offered me a drink several times before Sandrine put a glass of cucumber water in front of me.

Though he was rather an attack on the senses – his cologne was the third man in the room – Ronan managed to drive any thought of the murder from my mind, and for that I was grateful. I smiled along as he began to tell me his life story, but after I found out he was in the wine business, my gaze started to drift towards the other man, whom I now knew to be Sebastian Tombs.

He was lean, with a dignified air. He wore what I could only describe as a snazzy linen suit. Its cut was classic but fashion-able, understated but elegant. It suited his calm confidence, which drew out a curiosity inside me I was unable to resist. Who was this man? He had said no more than five words since I came in, but he made me feel as though we were old friends. He smiled as if he had an amusing secret he might or might not share, and the mystery around him was growing by the minute. He was a good-looking man, but it was the air of enigma that made him really attractive.

Of course, with Ronan babbling on, there wasn't much chance for him to say anything. Ronan had only reached teenage years in his epic retelling, so I sipped my water and tried to empty my mind, wishing I could be more like Beau, probably lying down on that plush bed upstairs, counting sheep, or enjoying the bath tea...

8

But then there was Céline

Staring at his phone screen, Beau paced the room again. He had been doing so since he arrived but hadn't got any closer to a decision. He looked at the situation from every angle he could think of, but it never made sense. He was convinced Franck was behind this murder somehow, but no matter how often he replayed the conversation with his uncle before Julie joined them, he could find no hint of what was about to happen.

He must be the worst double agent in history. Triple agent? He didn't even know any more. Everyone said they needed him, but nobody really trusted him. Except perhaps Julie. But judging from the way she'd looked at him at lunch, even she wasn't sure about him.

He stopped pacing at the foot of the bed, turned, and let himself fall. Then he held his phone up and gave in to the one thing he really wanted to do.

'Hey, gorgeous.'

The screen remained dark with a hint of movement, but Céline's voice was clear. 'Are you all right? Where are you?'

'Sandrine Lardy's place.'

The movement stopped just as the screen was getting slightly lighter. 'Why?'

'She invited Julie and me so we wouldn't have to stay in a hotel after what happened.'

'Oh. *C'est sympa, ça.*' The screen finally cleared and Céline's face came into view. She'd moved from the bakery to the living room at the back. 'So are you okay? People haven't stopped talking about you two for hours. First we didn't know why the police would be at Julie's, but you know, we all know her, so we already thought there'd been another murder, but not like this. Terrible! How are you?'

Beau smiled. She'd summed up the village in two sentences. 'I'm okay, but I just wanted to talk to you.'

'Why? Is there anything I can do?'

'No, I just wanted to' – see your face. Touch your hair. Kiss you madly – 'talk. Add some normality into the crazy. You're the most normal person I know.' It wasn't a lie. The most amazing, but also the most normal.

'Err, thanks? So what kind of normal would you like to hear?'

Tell me you love me half as much as I love you. He closed his eyes, only for a moment. That kind of thought wasn't helping him any.

'Oh, Thibault, I'm so sorry you had to go through that. I wish I could come and give you a hug. I wish there was anything I could do to help. Do you want me to close the shop?'

'No, of course not.'

'I would, you know. There's hardly anyone here, anyway. Everyone's staying indoors with this heat. But even if it was packed, I'd send them all home if you needed me.'

'I do need you.' She always coloured so sweetly when he said things like that. But she never reciprocated. 'Don't close the shop on my account, though. You can help me decide like this. I've been mulling over whether I should call my family or Jacqueline.'

'Ah.' She thought about that. Probably going through the same pros and cons he had. Well, not exactly the same, as she didn't know everything, but in broad strokes, she could reason with him.

Beau's family was on the other side of the law from Jacqueline, though she had recently quit the force. The family member Beau would be calling was undoubtedly his mother. His father never considered Beau a serious candidate to follow in his footsteps, which Beau had never regretted. But talking to his father about a murder he suspected his uncle had committed... The loyalties there got a little too tangled for Thibault's liking. Patrick Fouquet had publicly distanced himself from his brother when Franck was released from prison, and immediately afterwards, Thibault had been shot. The bullet only pierced his motorcycle helmet, and Franck had always denied any responsibility, but there had been a rift in the family ever since. A rift Thibault had had to bridge as well as he could manage without being obvious about it.

Ordinarily, the bond between him and his father would easily have outweighed that between him and his uncle. But it was on his uncle's orders that he'd come to live with Julie in the first place. *Keep an eye on her.* He'd done that, all right. He'd been navigating between spying on Julie and keeping her out of trouble for months. When his dad was openly against Franck, he'd even had to keep his contact with Franck a secret from his own family, as well as from Julie. Life had got ridiculously complicated.

After Beau had found out that someone else was to blame for much of the unrest in his father's ranks, Franck had managed to ingratiate himself with Patrick again, albeit up to a point. At least, he'd resumed his job at the cleaning products factory Patrick owned as a front. Since Patrick was never actually there, it had made communication with Franck that little bit easier, but Beau still didn't know exactly where the various members of his family thought he stood in the general order of the organisation.

Naturally, Céline was unaware of all this. She only knew what Julie knew: Thibault had 'escaped' his family, and now lived blissfully away from them all as a humble photographer's assistant. Which also just happened to be in the same village where the girl he'd loved since childhood ran her father's bakery. But she didn't know that either.

'I think you should at least let your mum know you're okay,' Céline finally said. 'And as for Jacqueline... You mean you want to talk to Ken, right?'

She had him there. If he didn't go out of his way to hide things from her, she always knew. Ken Doo was about to return to America to shoot his next blockbuster, and Jacqueline would be joining him. Though Thibault had only known Ken and his famous friends for a short time, the way they'd been talking about their films and their lives as actors had stoked a little fire inside him. He'd never considered acting a valid option as a career before. It had always been more of a survival skill in his family, to make others believe you fit in. But Julie had praised his talent in that department from the start. Little did she know...

Now, Beau would have to make a decision. Ken had invited him to come along to Los Angeles so he could introduce him to the right people. It could be the start of something magnificent. Something completely different, and hopefully lucrative without being dishonest. Leaving his family and all their drama behind only deepened his desire to go.

But then there was Céline.

Could he live without her, even if she'd only ever wanted to be his friend? Should he risk telling her how he felt? He'd already made that mistake once. When they were seventeen. She'd laughed in his face as if it was the best joke ever. He'd left her alone for a while after that. Tried to do without her, found different friends, made stupid mistakes. But in the end, he couldn't stay away. When Uncle Franck ordered him to Saint-Maurice, he'd leapt at the chance.

Of course he'd go to wherever Céline was. Even if it was under the pretence of watching Julie. He was the only one in the family Julie might trust, so it made sense that they'd send him. Beau's family might not think much of him, but they knew he could handle women. And what was Julie to them but just another woman? What had Julie been to him but just another woman? All right, he had a soft spot for her. When she was still married to Uncle Franck, she'd been pretty much the only one interested in Beau's drawings and what they meant to him. In fact, she'd thought more of them than he himself did, but at least she listened to him.

Leaving her now to go to America had never really seemed like an obstacle. Not nearly as much as leaving Céline. Julie had built up her own business and was making good money. She had her family and friends right there with her in that boring village. She would be fine without him. Of course, it stung a little that she'd already found his replacement before he'd even told her about his plans. That Chantelle was a little too eager to take his place.

But the real problem was this murder. If Franck was now ready to kill a random woman just to get to Julie, how could Beau leave her to his mercy, just to pursue a possible career?

'I do want to talk to Ken. He, err... asked if I might like to come along. To Los Angeles. I thought I might go.' His stomach clenched. He would have preferred to tell her in person. Gauging her reaction on a phone screen was a lot more difficult.

She raised her eyebrows. 'Oh! I thought you would have said yes already. Why haven't you?'

Because of you! How could she know everything that went on in his mind and not realise how much she meant to him? But all he could do is find an excuse again. 'That's why I want to talk to Jacqueline first. Maybe she can tell me whether they need me for this murder investigation.'

Céline frowned at the camera. 'Why would they need you?'

'Because of Franck.'

'What's Franck got to do with it?'

'He killed that woman, of course.'

She gasped, and her eyes widened. 'Really? Is he in jail again?'

'Well, no, I guess they have to process the fingerprints first, or something.'

Céline took a breath to say something but then let it go again. A second later, she took another breath. 'Hang on. They're not sure he did it?'

Beau shrugged. 'I don't know. But he was there. Everyone else was inside, enjoying the party. You think some random person would have the key to Julie's house *and* to her gate, and use *her* shoe to kill *her* guest?'

'No... But it doesn't make sense for Franck to do that either, does it?'

Beau threw up his hand. 'Who knows what makes sense to Franck.'

Having dealt with a number of Franck's whims over the past few months, Beau uttered those words with conviction.

'But then you can't be sure he did it.'

It sounded reasonable enough, but... 'I know I'm right.'

Céline shook her head. 'It's been a shocking day, Thibault. First that bump on your head, and now a murder in your home. I think you should have an early night. Tomorrow, things will look different.'

He stared at his screen. She hadn't made any comment about his plans to move away. Did she not realise he'd be gone? Did she not care?

'Thanks. I'll do that. See you tomorrow?'

'Count on it.' She blew him a kiss and hung up.

Beau dropped his hand to the bed, and the phone skipped away. What did he expect? She had lived in Saint-Maurice for years. She had her friends here, and her job. He hadn't asked her to come with him. And why would she come, if he was just another friend?

He picked up the phone, sat up, and called Ken. He couldn't stay. It would kill him.

'So, have you decided?' Ken was outside somewhere, his long, blond hair hidden underneath a baseball cap. He looked more American than ever.

'I think so. But, err, have you heard?'

Jacqueline's face slid into view. 'We heard.'

'So does that change things? Do I need to stay?'

'Depends. Did you kill that woman?'

'Very funny.'

'Tell us what happened.'

A tree appeared in the background and remained there, so Jacqueline and Ken had probably found a quiet place to listen. Beau told them the whole story, starting from the arrival of

Franck but omitting the conversation he'd had with him before Julie came to the door.

'So I thought, maybe because I'm the killer's family, I need to—'

'You think Franck did it?' Jacqueline interrupted.

Beau paused. 'Isn't it obvious?' Céline might have doubted him, but he had expected Jacqueline to be in his corner.

'Is it? I'd say it's a bit too obvious to be true.'

'Aren't you the one always saying that the solution with the fewest question marks is probably the right one? He was there, he hates Julie—'

'Yes, but why this lady? That's a massive question mark. Franck has only ever dealt with white-collar crimes. And now he violently murders a random woman? That doesn't fit his profile.'

Beau huffed. 'That's a bunch of impersonal psychology. I know him.'

'You also don't like him. Don't let your bias cloud your judgement.'

'I just want to know if I can leave.' The more he thought about it, the more he wanted nothing more to do with any of it – his family, his boss, this dumb village that seemed to attract trouble like children to sharp objects.

Jacqueline and Ken exchanged a look. Great, now he was being judged on abandoning his friends. What had these 'friends' ever done for him?

'Unless they tell you not to, you're free to go,' Jacqueline answered flatly.

'Good, then I'm going.'

'Excellent!' Ken chimed in. You could always count on him to shine a light on the positive side. 'I've already got several people I want you to meet. I'll get you a ticket as soon as we're home.'

Beau thanked him, ended the call, and let himself fall back onto the bed. If he was leaving, there was one more thing he should probably do. He wasn't looking forward to it, but he'd hate himself if he didn't call *her*.

9

Not everyone is a local

Ronan had just come to the part of his story where he got into the wine business when Emile Lardy sauntered in. I'd only seen him once or twice before, at village fetes like the *nuits de rosé*. Though there was nothing particularly noteworthy about his appearance, the way he carried himself made me think he'd be into secret handshakes. Still, I thought I might like him once I got to know him. He raised his chin to Lips, who was reading a fashion magazine in a corner of the room, then joined our little group, taking a seat on the third couch, the only unoccupied one. I had been wishing I'd taken that seat instead of sitting down next to Ronan for at least half an hour now.

Sebastian was still politely nodding along, but I'd zoned out, only occasionally checking in to see if Ronan had found something interesting to say yet. Unfortunately, his ability to take my mind off the day's events had long since dwindled, but I also couldn't concentrate well enough to actually get anywhere thinking about the who and why of the murder. I wished I was in my room, so I could try pulling out my negative thoughts like I'd done so many times before, though I doubted this time it would work.

'Dinner soon,' Emile Lardy broke into the constant stream of words. 'Any preference for wine?'

Ronan didn't seem in the least offended that he'd been interrupted. 'Though we're squarely in Beaujolais Villages country here, it'll have to be one of your excellent Crus du Beaujolais, won't it? How about a rosé? Any will do.'

I frowned, but Emile nodded, so he must know something I didn't. I had heard through the grapevine – i.e., my mother, the mayor of Saint-Maurice – that Emile had invested in Domaine de Montmales. I'd met its owner, the Vicomtesse de Montmales, around the same time I'd met Sandrine, when we were all stranded at the château in a blizzard. Emile was supposed to be there too, but he'd dropped out at the last moment, leaving Sandrine to fend for herself. Despite all that had happened, Emile had seen an opportunity and had gone into business with the vicomtesse.

'Do you know la Vicomtesse de Montmales?' The cultured voice of Sebastian Tombs startled me. Had he read my thoughts?

'I do. Why?' I couldn't help but ask.

'Oh, pardon me, I thought perhaps Sandrine might have told you. She's joining us for dinner this evening. I'm very much looking forward to meeting her.'

A smile crept over my lips. If civility was a binding factor, Sebastian Tombs and Hélène Blanc-Mattieu would get along swimmingly. She had an almost regal air about her, and he could well be of noble blood himself.

'It may seem an odd thing to say about someone you don't know all that well, but I'm quite fond of her,' I admitted. 'I admire her strength and her sense of justice.'

Sebastian cocked his head. 'Do you? That's an unusual character trait to laud.'

'But mostly I like her because she made me feel welcome in her home,' I added quickly, not wanting to get into details of the circumstances in which we met. 'The castle may be centuries old, but she made it a warm and inviting place.'

'I heard they do weddings there,' Ronan chimed in, and I nodded.

'Yes, it's a beautiful venue. In every season.' I didn't know why I felt the need to praise Vicomtesse Hélène, as I hadn't seen her in months, but both other guests seemed interested. 'I hear you've done very well together,' I addressed Emile.

Emile didn't answer immediately. He hung back in the couch sipping his cucumber water, his ankle crossed over his knee. 'Yes,' he drawled eventually. 'But I'll let her tell you about our venture. *Bonsoir, ma dame.*'

Vicomtesse Hélène had entered the room together with Sandrine. They were followed by Pupils, who veered towards

Lips and sat on the floor next to her chair, doing nothing. Sandrine curled up on the couch next to her husband, and Hélène approached the two foreigners, who'd got up from their seats to shake her hand.

She took the remaining seat next to Sebastian and brushed a hand over her carmine silk skirt. As always, she was impeccably dressed, her loose, cream-coloured blouse showing no wrinkles, contrary to my yellow linen top. But she never made me feel inferior. She simply gave me a warm greeting, then turned to Emile.

'I've told you before, Emile, call me Hélène. And I wouldn't want to bring down the tone of the conversation by talking about business.' She glanced my way, and I was grateful to her.

'Are you in the wine business too, then, Monsieur Tombs?' I asked him.

'You could say that,' he replied in a modest tone that indicated he was not, in fact, a small player. 'I represent a third party with a vested interest.'

None of the others batted an eyelid, but I couldn't ask for more details, as Sandrine's housekeeper announced dinner. We all sat down to eat and kept the conversation light. I noticed Thibault didn't look much more rested than he had when we arrived, but as he was on the other end of the table, I couldn't talk to him without shouting. I was seated between Sebastian Tombs and Hélène Blanc-Mattieu, who sat at Emile Lardy's right hand as he presided over the table like the CEO he was. Ronan Kelly was opposite Hélène and, on that same side of the table, Beau was flanked by the blondes, with Lips next to Ronan. Sandrine had taken the seat on Sebastian's right.

As Sebastian was in conversation with Sandrine and Emile kept Hélène occupied, I busied myself with studying the others, if only to keep the image of Delphine lying on my porch out of my mind. The cold vegetable soup in front of me was suited to the hot weather but rather bland in taste, and I only finished it out of politeness. Ronan, however, was slurping it down.

My gaze flicked between him and Emile, wondering whether the Irishman realised how much he did not fit in with the rest of the company. Well, he and his ladies. I got the feeling that not only did he know, but he relished and embellished the difference. Hélène and Sebastian both possessed the level of sophistication only achieved by years of civilised dinners with people you hardly know but have to keep on good terms with for propriety's sake. My mother had taught me the rules and manners and ways of that world, and though I'd kicked myself out of it years ago, I could still behave correctly. The Lardys were obviously centuries late to the party but had adjusted admirably. Beau, of course, came from a very different background, but he had learnt to act along with others from a very young age.

But Kelly and the blondes, they didn't show mild interest, didn't speak softly on subjects nobody had any particular opinion on, didn't take the tiniest of bites. The blondes seemed to have been instructed to keep quiet. Several times, I caught Lips surreptitiously imitating Hélène. She, at least, was trying to fit in. But poor Pupils had given up. Her eyes had returned to normal, but now she was listlessly stirring her soup. She showed no interest at all in my handsome assistant, who had attempted conversation on both sides but got no response and was now eating in silence, not his usual self at all.

But Ronan seemed to enjoy his position. He talked loudly, to no one in particular, about football, cars, and Irish politics. As I was the only one in his vicinity not already in conversation, I assumed he was addressing me, but with nothing to say on any of those topics, all I could do was nod along, as I had done earlier.

At long last, well into the third course, Emile turned to him and asked if he had any plans for sightseeing while he was in the area. I almost sighed with relief.

The vicomtesse took the opportunity to catch up. 'It's a lovely surprise to see you here, Julie. Are you a friend of the Lardys, or is this a business occasion?'

I hesitated. She obviously hadn't heard the news. And as I didn't want to explain, I said simply, 'I'm here at the kind invitation of Madame Lardy.'

'And she couldn't have chosen a better person to spend this evening with. How is your mother? And Monsieur Le Roux? I believe I have seen them together on several occasions?'

I gave her a smile I couldn't entirely keep from containing a little schadenfreude, as the relationship between my mother and the mayor of Hélène's village still bugged my younger brother David. He found the man too loud and boisterous. 'They are both well, thank you. And I've heard good news from your side as well. All true, I hope?'

As expected, Hélène's smile started out a little sad, but she soon recovered. 'Much of that is due to Emile. After... the events at which you were present, it became clear that he had already decided to do business with our estate. I have had to step up and learn quickly, but it has been... an interesting journey.' She glowed as she pronounced those words. No longer the withdrawn Lady of the Castle, the change had undoubtedly done her good. 'Do you remember Sacha Toledo? We published a history of the château together, her urbex pictures alongside historical documents from our records. I could not believe how popular that proved to be. Not only with the public, but with academics and investors too.'

She smiled at Emile, who was still talking to Ronan. 'Of course, by then, I already had a business partner. When Emile learned we grow Pinot Liébault grapes for some of our wines, he became doubly interested and has taken over production and marketing of those wines completely. *Entre nous*, it took me a while to get used to the idea, but he has taught me so much that I now have my hands full with all our other wines, and I'm actually grateful that he concerns himself with those.'

'Of course, you are born and bred here,' Sebastian chimed in from my other side, 'but I looked quite green when I first came to the Beaujolais and had to ask what Pinot Liébault was.'

Amused, I smiled. 'Oh, it's just a local variation of Pinot Noir. Like Pinot Gris is called Pinot Beurot.'

'Obviously, I know that *now*.' He tilted his head towards me and raised an eyebrow. 'But not everyone is a local.'

'And most Beaujolais wines come from Gamay grapes,' Hélène reassured him. 'Only a few use other grape varieties to mix in. You'd have to really know your Beaujolais to know of these names.'

I was about to ask how long ago it had been that he'd made this mistake, as I'd understood he had a respectable amount of experience in the business, but I was cut off by Ronan.

'Mark my words, they'll never find that guy.' He, apparently, had no qualms about shouting across the table to be heard because it was Sandrine who answered.

'Do you have information the police are missing, Monsieur Kelly?'

'Ronan, please. And no, but he's been missing for weeks. These underworld types, when they go missing, they're gone.

And this Michel Seive, didn't he have some sort of mafia rebellion going on that was quelled?'

'That was indeed what I was commending Thibault on. He provided the evidence that was supposed to help convict Monsieur Seive before he disappeared.'

The unthinkable happened. Ronan had nothing to say. He leaned forward over his food to get a better look at Beau. 'Did he now?' was all he said. He remained remarkably quiet throughout the rest of the meal, while Sebastian kept me in conversation, asking me about growing up in the Beaujolais and comparing it to his own childhood in the British countryside. All in all, I spent a pleasant evening, but I couldn't wait to call Léon and let everything out that had happened today.

Once in my room, I immediately took out my phone and called him, unable to wait for him to call me as he usually did. It took him a long while to answer and I was about to give up when his sweet face appeared.

'Hello, my lovely. Couldn't wait, could you? Just a few more days, and I'll be with you again.'

Smiling, I closed my eyes and let that notion fill me for a second. Only a few more days, and I could kiss him again! He'd come to stay with me for one weekend over the few months we'd been apart, and we'd made up for the single kiss we'd shared before he went away, but I'd had to make do with daily video calls and no kisses again for too long now. I needed him here with me, so I could physically lean on him. I never thought that would be so important to me. Just a few more days of waiting now.

'I know. But they will be very long days. Especially with what happened today.' I wiggled down on the pillows and related every bit of what had happened, from meeting Capucine in the morning to having to send her home with one less friend, and everything in between. Léon listened with growing concern. He knew all about my past with Franck. He'd been almost in the middle of it. He knew exactly how terrifying it was to now have that man appear back in my life, along with a dead body 'in my back yard', as he put it.

'But you are not at home now. Where are you?'

'One of my former clients, Sandrine? I think I told you about her.' He nodded. 'She invited me to stay as long as I wished. Beau's here too. And some other people her husband is doing business with. The police kicked us out of the house. And I just couldn't stay in a hotel tonight, Léon, it was so awful! I keep seeing her face with the big...' I swallowed and gestured at my temple, indicting a small explosion with my hand.

Seeing my beautiful man look so helplessly at the camera, trying to find words to soothe me, actually soothed me without him saying anything. I smiled bravely for him. *Merci, mon chéri.*

'I didn't say anything.'

'You didn't have to.' I sighed. 'Can't wait to see you.'

'Not long now.'

I asked him about his day to distract me. He still tried to find ways to calm me but then realised distraction would help me most, so he talked until I started nodding off. Then he blew me a kiss and I fell into a heavy sleep.

10

I'd like to put on some pants

'What did you think of that rosé?' I asked Beau the next morning. I had waited impatiently for signs of life before I opened the connecting door between our rooms.

'Ever heard of knocking?' He was still in bed, rubbing the sleep out of his eyes. He raised his knee, which pulled the sheet down his bare chest.

'Knock, knock. The rosé?'

'Who's there,' he mumbled, then made an effort to wake up. We'd retired early the night before. At dinner, Beau hadn't said much, which was almost a first for him. Usually, he sparkled in company, but the dullness of his conversation attested to his exhaustion.

'Err, nice?' He sat up and draped his arm over his knee. Why do you want to know about the rosé? They're wine people, of course the wine will be good.'

'Yes, but it was a Beaujolais Villages, right?'

He blinked, probably hoping he could wipe me from his sight that way, but I was going to make my point. 'I expect so. Are you going anywhere with this? I'd like to put on some pants if you're going to stay here.'

Irritatingly, I blushed, though I knew he was just messing with me. 'That Ronan Kelly asked for a Grand Cru rosé to be served at dinner.'

Now, he frowned. Ha! 'That doesn't exist.'

'*Merci beaucoup!* And he is supposed to be a wine person, as you called them.'

'Okay, so he doesn't know his stuff. What's it to you?'

I stared at him. 'Don't you think that's strange? Emile is a millionaire. He only does business with big players. So how has this guy become a big player if he doesn't know his Grand Crus from his Villages? And Emile didn't call him out, either. He just went along with it.'

Beau stretched and got out of bed, pants and all. Reaching for his shorts, he said, 'I think you're reading too much into this. Did you sleep at all or were you coming up with conspiracy theories all night?'

I followed the hem of his T-shirt going down over his stomach. His lack of interest was making me grumpy. 'I slept fine.'

Sandrine's house was quite a bit higher up than mine, and the air up here got much cooler overnight. I'd left the shutters open, which had made my bedroom wonderfully fresh. The only annoying thing was that the house across the valley had quite a bright light on at some point. The wind must have blown a curtain across it, or something, as its flickering had annoyed me during my call with Léon, but I'd fallen asleep before I could wonder any more about the rosé Grand Cru.

Beau's voice came from the en suite. 'Are you sure you're not just creating minor mysteries so you won't have to deal with the major one?'

When did he get so wise? 'No.' I sounded like a sulky teenager caught using her mother's expensive perfume. Not that I knew what that was like. I would never. Not me.

Beau reappeared. Slowly. I followed his gaze to the floor, but there was nothing of interest there.

'Julie, I've been thinking.'

Oh, not now! It was too soon! Panic heated my neck. I could feel it creeping up the back of my head. I still needed him with me to get through this murder mess. I couldn't do it alone.

'Maybe we should leave this one to the police.'

'What do you mean?' I squeezed out. He was going. He wouldn't be able to help me out.

He put his hand on the door frame, now staring at the bed. 'We're too involved. The other murders, we could help out because they had nothing to do with us. But this one... Even if it turns out some random crazy guy broke in and killed the first person in sight, they still did it in our home. And you know I don't believe that, anyway.'

Our home? No investigating? That was it? He wasn't leaving yet? All my anxiety washed away. I could almost feel it flush down my spine and along my legs, and I had the urge to lift and shake my foot to get rid of the last drops of it.

'You don't want to find out who killed Delphine?' I asked with a croaky voice that Beau misinterpreted.

'I do! Of course! But I think we should find out through the proper authorities. That Rouletabille seems to know what he's doing.'

I swallowed. This was fine. We'd just stay away from this whole business and wait until the police had cleared it up so we could go back to our normal lives. 'All right. Let's do that.'

The tension visibly left his body, and he smiled at me. 'How about some breakfast?'

We filed into the dark corridor, both full of relieved chatter. Deciding I'd help the housekeeper out, I opened the window at the end of the corridor, leaning over the wicker chair with the thick, messy throw on it to open the shutters and let the light in. After the start I'd just had, I drank in the morning air, though the tractor spraying the vineyard next door had me cease that activity instantly. Such an expensive house, and still within a hundred metres of a vineyard. Shame.

Wiping my damp, dewy fingers on my skirt, I closed the window again. Today was going to be sticky. If there was anything I needed to do, I'd better do it soon, before the heat had us all taking extra-long *siestes*. Fortunately, I'd planned no shoots for the coming month. The party was my last work effort before Léon arrived in a couple of days. Ordinarily, I would have been working out the return on investment my party had given me, but that activity didn't draw me in the least. I should probably be happy if I had any clients left if word got out that one of them had been murdered. I groaned, and Beau looked up.

'Sorry. I just realised what impact this whole thing could have on my business.'

'What, already?'

I swatted his arm. 'I'm sorry! I was a little too busy figuring out what its impact was on *me*. And you, for that matter. But it looks like you're back to normal already. I seem to have ruined your innocence.'

He laughed. 'What innocence? Have you met my family?'

'How is your mum?' Thibault's mother was the only one in his family, apart from Beau himself, that I liked. There were a few others I wasn't necessarily against, but Colette Fouquet cared about me. She'd apologised for the way I'd been treated, even though that was not her fault. 'Is she all right? Was she worried?'

Beau hung his head.

'You didn't call her! I thought you were going to when you stayed behind in your room.'

'I was. I... sent her a text.'

'Oh, what a good son. Call her!' We'd come to the dining room, but I blocked his way in.

'It's too early,' he whined.

'She'll be up. And even if she's not, you know she'll want to hear from you. Do you remember how frantic she was when you got shot?'

'Shot *at*. My helmet got shot.'

I waved an impatient hand, and my tone got angrier. 'Call her.'

He paused for a breath. 'After breakfast?'

Narrowing my eyes at him, I suddenly realised I was spending what could be my last days with him arguing, so I stepped aside and we entered together. The large, rectangular table was populated at both ends today, but no one had taken the places in the middle. Ronan and his blondes were on our left, looking like they hadn't slept much. To the right, Sandrine and Sebastian were talking quietly. She stood when she saw us come in.

'Ah, *mes chéris*, how are you feeling? Did you sleep well? Would you like some coffee?' Despite her grand, dramatic tone, I now realised she meant well, so I smiled.

'Yes, thank you. Apart from your neighbours' bright light, I had a wonderful night's sleep and I'm feeling much better.'

The full cup stilled and hovered when it should have come to my outstretched, greedy hand.

'What, the house across the valley? But that's been empty for months.'

I frowned at her. 'Are you sure? There was a big light on somewhere that shone into my room. Where else could it have come from?'

Sandrine narrowed her eyes, and even Sebastian was following our conversation with interest.

'We don't have any lights on at night. I haven't seen anything, but our room is on the other side. Perhaps it was a car?'

I thought about that. 'I don't think so. The light was bright enough, but it kept switching off, like the wind was blowing a curtain or a shutter across it, or something.'

'But there hasn't been any wind in days with this heatwave. Not even up here,' Sebastian said.

I stared at him. That hadn't occurred to me yet. Why would someone leave on a strong, flickering light?

Slicing an apple, Sandrine had already lost interest. 'I'll have a look tonight, if it's still on. Perhaps someone rented the house and they were moving around in front of this light. I wouldn't want to do the heavy lifting of a house move in the middle of the day right now either.'

Sebastian nodded, and so did Beau. Munching on a fresh croissant, I considered Sandrine's explanation. It actually made much more sense than the curtain flapping in a non-existent breeze in an abandoned house. What had I been thinking?

'So, do you have plans for today? You're welcome to just stay here and relax, if that's what you prefer.'

Wondering why Sandrine had hidden this warm side of hers before, I smiled at her. Was it just that she was more at ease in her own home and didn't have to pretend? The self-important diva I'd met before was so far removed from the woman she was now that I was beginning to wonder why she'd given up acting. Or perhaps the new woman was an act?

Buttering another croissant, I stole a glance at Beau, who dipped his in his coffee. Maybe he could tell the difference, as he was forever pretending to be someone he wasn't.

'Fortunately, my schedule is clear for the foreseeable future, so I won't have to be in my studio until they've cleaned it.' Wait, was Beau going to call the cleaners, or was I supposed to have done that? 'My business partner asked me to cover for her at the hotel, so I'm going to keep myself busy there.'

'Excellent. And again, do let me know if there's anything I can do.'

'You're already doing it.'

She acknowledged me with a smile. Again, I glanced at Beau, but he was still engrossed in dunking his food in his drink. That was a habit I never did understand. Donuts, sure. They're dry. But croissants? They're so deliciously melty already, why would you drown that in coffee? Still, I kept staring unseeingly at my assistant. Perhaps he would have a brilliant idea of how to repay Sandrine, because I could think of nothing but to accept her kindness for the moment.

I took a breath and refocused. Jeanette had sent me a text early that morning saying she knew I must have a tonne on my mind but could I please fill in for her at the hotel? She didn't want to leave a sick Théo by himself and if she did, she wouldn't be worth anything if she kept thinking about him. At first, I'd thought to hand over the reins to Jeanette's second in command, like I'd done the day before. But, thinking about it, a day's work at the hotel might provide the solid distraction I craved.

Every time my thoughts stalled, that horrific image came to the forefront of my mind again. Perhaps Beau was right. Perhaps I'd made a thing of the light last night so I wouldn't have to think about anything else. But now that mystery had been solved, my thoughts kept wandering to the woman in my courtyard.

But I'd noticed they now started to creep in another direction too. My imagination was playing out what had happened before we found Delphine. As much as I tried not to, I kept seeing Franck with my shoe in his hand, sneaking up on her. Raising his hand. And...

I pushed off from the table. 'I'd better go. I'll see you later?'

Beau looked up and nodded. He had no business at the hotel, unless Céline happened to be there, but she had no business there, either. Good, I decided. The fewer people there that I had to talk to, the better.

11

What was he doing in my hotel?

'Julie! How are you?'

'Oh, Julie, are you all right?'

'You *poor* thing! You simply *must* tell me all about it.' That was Bella Dudevant, of course. My village nemesis *would* find a way to make this about her. I'd been dodging people's questions and well-wishes all morning. For some reason, they all expected me to solve this murder, when there was a perfectly good police force on it. But not Bella. She was already tittering about a job interview she'd had when Beau strolled in.

Bella had opened her purse and was going through it. 'Hold this.' She shoved a water bottle in my hands. 'Hold this.' Her wallet got pushed into the hands of a passing waiter, who raised his eyebrows but diligently waited for her to take it off him again. 'And you hold me while I fall apart.'

She daintily dropped herself in Beau's arms as he was passing. Credit where credit is due: he caught her beautifully. He'd make a wonderful film hero. But I could only shake my head at

Bella's... flirtation. The first word that had come to mind was attack, which it might have been to anyone but Beau.

'Rough morning, Bella?' he asked as he planted her firmly back on her feet.

She giggled as she straightened her hair. 'So I met with this lady for a job interview. She was stylish and all, but she had one long hair on her ankle that she'd missed shaving a couple of times. Now, bushy or bald, I don't care much, but that one quill really bothered me.'

While her out-of-the-blue confession left me nonplussed, Beau appeared unfazed. 'So did you get the job?'

She shrugged. 'Nah, she didn't like me.' And with that, she plucked her water bottle and wallet from various hands and wandered off.

'I wonder why,' Beau pondered.

The waiter tried to hide a smile, then went on with his duties.

I took a breath, opened my mouth, closed my eyes, pressed my lips together as I opened my eyes again, and then just laughed. 'I can't even.'

Beau grinned.

'So what are you doing here?' I asked him.

His expression sobered. 'You were right to keep yourself busy. I thought it would help to do nothing and relax, but my thoughts are just going round and round in circles. So now I'm going to sit here and do nothing, but at least I'll have something to watch.'

That he did. Since Jeanette had closed the café, the hotel had taken over its social function, and people were in and out of the lobby all day. I walked Beau over to the sitting area and joined the barman at the espresso machine.

'Hey, do you want ice cream?' Beau asked.

'I'm making coffee.' When no answer came, I turned and gestured at the machine to underline my words.

He raised his eyebrows. 'I take it that's a no, then?'

'Obviously.'

'It's not that obvious. Ever heard of affogato?'

I narrowed my eyes at him, and two minutes later, we were both spooning vanilla ice cream from its little coffee bath.

'I don't want to keep you from your work...' he began.

I huffed. 'Gaëlle is very good at her job. If Jeanette doesn't give her a raise after this, I will.' I flapped my hand to wave away his mock concerns. 'I'm just here as a flagship.'

'A very small one.'

'I'd like to see you walk in these, all right?' I pointed at my stiletto sandals, but as soon as I did, we both winced and sat in silence for a while. Though we were in a public space, we'd chosen chairs at the edge, and I decided my method was worth a try. I put my finger and thumb to my temple, closed my eyes to work extra hard to collect all my negative thoughts, and pulled. Nothing happened. I pulled a few more times, but all I accomplished was that the image of Delphine lying on my porch appeared more clearly at the forefront of my mind.

'Do you really think it was him?' I asked at last, abandoning my attempts.

He slowly shook his head and held up a hand. 'I don't know who else...' His gaze darkened, and he frowned in the direction of the entrance.

Alarmed, I turned in my seat. Just inside the revolving door was Franck, lazily looking about the place. In spite of all my therapy and self-confidence reminders, my first reaction to the sight of him was still to shiver. But – win of the day – that was immediately followed by a flare of annoyance. What was he doing in *my* hotel? Had he not caused enough trouble?

Slowly, I turned back to Beau. 'If he did do it... this is a pretty brazen move.'

He nodded, still with his eyes on Franck. 'The whole thing was brazen. Murdering someone while we were having a party on the other side of the wall.'

I rose. None of the staff would know who Franck was. It came down to me to kick him out. Drawing myself up as tall and straight as I would get, I approached him but couldn't keep the hiss from my voice when I asked, 'What are you doing here?'

'*Chérie*, this is a public place, is it not?'

'It is, but I am not your *chérie*, and I have the right to refuse you access to *my* building.'

He gave a leisurely smile that had me dig my nails into the palms of my hands. 'On what grounds?'

'I don't need any grounds. But as it happens, I think the murder that was committed on my property, coincidentally right around the time you were there, would be grounds enough for anyone.'

His genuine shock threw me. 'A wh— a murder? In your house?'

I frowned, still only half believing what I saw. 'It was all over the news.' People had been showing me their phones with various pictures of my house, along with portraits of me and of Delphine, since I'd walked into the hotel, so it was highly unlikely that Franck could have missed it.

He shook his head with a frown that I used to think made him look brooding and attractive but now meant nothing to me. 'I don't look at the news much since... well... in the last few years. It's hardly ever to do with me. And believe it or not, I don't have many friends any more who would tell me about something like this. Not since Cyprien disappeared.'

He looked me in the eye. 'But you have to believe that it *is* just that: a coincidence. I was only there to apologise to you. Why would I kill anyone? I didn't know them. I didn't even know you had people over, or I would have come another time.'

I kept quiet and stared at him with as angry a look as I could muster, which was pretty angry.

'Please, Julie. One coffee, that's all. Then I'll go.'

When I didn't react, he turned and started for the bar. Beau raised his head and glared at me, then wrinkled his nose and shook his head in confusion. I bit my lips and shrugged, palms up. Franck was right, this was supposed to be a public place.

Beau came up to me. 'Why didn't you throw him out?'

'I don't know, I... I think he really didn't know about the murder.'

'Of course he knew about the murder!' he whispershouted. 'He committed it.'

'We don't *know* that.'

Beau growled, throwing his head back in frustration.

Pretending it was my decision to let Franck stay instead of being overruled again, I added, 'And if he did, as long as he's here, we can keep an eye on him. See if he gives himself away.'

'He's drinking coffee. How is he going to give himself away?'

'Well, anyway, he's only here for one coffee. How hard can it be to survive that long?'

One coffee had lasted him an hour and a half. Beau had already left, and the staff had started to consider him part of the furniture after they'd repeatedly tried to take his coffee away or ask him if he'd like a new one, and he'd refused. I couldn't concentrate on anything to do with the hotel while he was here, so I promised myself again I'd give acting manager Gaëlle a raise. Instead, I'd given in to people wanting to chat to me and had planted myself at one of the coffee tables surrounded by comfy chairs, at the other end of the area from where Franck sat scrolling on his phone but with a full view of him. Unfortunately, that meant I only picked up half the conversations I was having.

My best friend Tiana had rounded up Nienke and Marie to talk about our experience of the previous day, but as we talked, I noticed my friends' tone get lighter, and eventually they forgot about the subject at hand completely and went on to other topics. While I was happy for them that they could work through this so easily, with the possible killer sitting right in front of me, I couldn't possibly let go of my fears and suspicions.

'Well used but serviceable. Like my boobs.' The sentence barely registered, and I didn't know who had uttered it.

'Mine are just old. But maybe if I call them vintage, they'll get a second life.' That was definitely Nienke. The others sniggered.

'At least you've still got your slender figure,' Marie said. 'I never had one of those. When they designed me, they coloured outside the lines. Especially my hips. But the extra padding is actually quite useful. My hips are for carrying. Laundry baskets, trays of eggs, stacks of books... Anything the kids leave lying about the house, really.'

They laughed again, but I was distracted by Franck coughing and looking my way, and the others fell quiet. After a few seconds, Marie and Nienke reached for their purses and got up.

'Well, I'd better...'

'Yes, I should go too. Lots of... you know. *Á plus, les filles.*' Marie waved, and Tiana smiled.

As soon as they'd left, she turned to me. 'Okay, tell me. Why is he here? Why do you keep glaring at him instead of kicking him out? Do you want me to...?'

I shook my head. 'He's not doing anything wrong. He's just... there. He said he'd only drink the one coffee and then he'd leave. It must be stone cold by now, but he keeps telling the waiter he's not finished.'

'You do realise he's playing you again, right? Always finding the little loopholes to make you think he's right and you're wrong. Sound familiar?'

My gaze snapped from him to her. She was right. My stomach roiled at the realisation, and I almost retched. Gasping for breath, I stood, only to have to sit down again and let the red clear from my vision. Tiana's hand on my arm had a calming effect, but I still stood straight back up and marched over to Franck's table. He looked up with his trademark disarming smile.

For once, I wasn't affected. 'All right, enough is enough. You are—'

'Franck Fouquet?' a somewhat familiar voice next to me inquired. I turned my head and recognised Major Étienne Chagrin, who had apparently just entered the lobby while I was focused on Franck. 'When did you last speak to Cyprien Gréban?'

The smile turned into a confused frown. 'Cyprien? I haven't seen him in weeks. Why?'

'I'm afraid he has been found dead this morning.'

Both Franck and I gasped. Not another death. Though I'd be the last person to mourn Cyprien, this second unexpected death in two days came as a shock.

'We suspect foul play,' the officer added with no small amount of self-importance.

I reached for the back of the chair next to me and leaned heavily against it. Yet another murder. How many more could I take?

'In fact, a man matching your description was seen leaving the scene not long before. Might I enquire as to your whereabouts this morning?'

Franck was visibly upset. His eyes darted all over, he didn't know what to do with his hands, and he stuttered. I'd never seen him like this before. Ever. 'Err... yes. Err... of course. I was... here. Actually. I was here. All morning. Just ask her. She owns the place.'

His last words were much more self-assured. If there was one thing he did well, it was to divert attention away from himself. And I was the most convenient of distractions.

I nodded, swallowing to make sure I could speak. 'He was here. From about eleven.'

'You were also on Madame Belmain's property yesterday, around three o'clock, were you not?' a new voice joined in. I glanced around Major Chagrin and discovered Brigadier-Chef Joseph Rouletabille.

'If that was the time, yes. I didn't pay much attention to the clock.'

'And you are aware of the events that followed your visit to Madame Belmain?'

'She informed me of them this morning. I have been sitting here, processing the news. And now you tell me there has been another death, and it concerns my dearest friend. If you don't mind, gentlemen, I'd like to come to terms with this horror in peace.' Though his tone was angry, his eyes filled with tears.

Chagrin was unimpressed. 'I'm sorry, but we do have a few questions. For instance, how—'

'You can ask them later. You know where to find me.' He jumped up and legged it out of the hotel.

'Shall I go after him, sir?' Rouletabille asked.

Chagrin, still blinking at the outburst, slowly came back to reality. 'We'll catch him later,' he declared. 'Madame Belmain, if you please, you are certain Franck Fouquet has been here all morning?'

'He hasn't moved from this spot. Believe me, I kept an eye on him.' And, I now realised, I had the full bladder to prove it. I'd been sipping drinks with friends, family, and acquaintances while keeping that eye on him, and I now really needed the loo. I hoped Chagrin wasn't planning on asking me many more questions.

'Why? Are you two acquainted?'

Seriously? 'As I told you yesterday, he is my ex-husband, who I helped send to prison for fraud. I don't know anything about Cyprien's death, though. Now, unless you have any updates on yesterday's crime, I do have a hotel to run.'

The policemen took their leave, and I hurried to the staff washroom. On my way, I passed the kitchen, where the sous-chef was scolding someone.

'No, no, iceberg is a fast food lettuce, or to support the weight of chicken in a Caesar salad. Good salads use darker lettuce, that you can fold onto your fork.'

The fragment reminded me of poor, sick Théo, but also that it was lunchtime. Upon my return to the foyer, I ran into Thibault again. 'Lunch?'

12

We're not sorry

'That is what I came here for,' Beau said.

'Good. I can recommend—'

'But not to eat here,' he interrupted me. 'I just saw Maëline in the square, and she invited us over.'

My brother's lodger had finally made the upgrade to being his girlfriend, and ever since she joined the family, she'd been instrumental in getting us together regularly in the big family mansion where they lived.

'Oh. Okay.' I had the strange sensation that it was odd for the owner of the restaurant to have lunch elsewhere while on duty as manager, but I quickly let go of that notion when I saw Gaëlle firmly in place at Jeanette's desk. 'Let's not be late, then.'

I grabbed my purse and sun hat from behind the reception desk and led the way out the revolving doors and into the midday heat. After my lungs had adjusted to the change in temperature, I donned my sunglasses and asked, 'Feeling better?'

'A bit,' he said but didn't expand.

'Did you talk to Céline today?'

He smiled half-heartedly. 'I mostly saw Frou-Frou. Whenever she's walking that dog, she only has eyes for him. Or her.'

'You regret giving her the dog?'

Now he really smiled. 'Never. The dog makes her happy, and I just can't get enough of seeing her happy.' Then his smile turned sour. 'She's like an eclair. All soft and sweet and airy, but after one taste, all you want is more. But for me, there is no more.'

My heart broke for him. My love was far away, but at least I knew he felt the same and would soon be in my arms again. Beau's love was breathing the same dusty air he was but stayed tantalisingly just out of reach.

Hoping to distract him, I said, 'So here's a bit of news: the police came in to tell Franck they'd found the murdered body of Cyprien. He said he hadn't seen him in weeks. *They* said someone resembling him had been seen at the scene of the crime, but this was while he was right there under my nose.'

Beau's jaw dropped. I might have sugar-coated the news of another death, but he needed the distraction, and I was still so full of this latest development that I judged he would live.

'Cyprien is dead?!' He closed his mouth, then frowned. 'And you're Franck's alibi. That's mighty convenient.'

I hummed agreement. 'It felt dodgy to me as well, but the fact remains that he couldn't have done it. He was right here. Definitely him. And also... he seemed genuinely shocked to learn of Cyprien's death. I'll be the first to admit I can't trust my judgement around him, but he was pretty convincing.'

We'd walked the short distance from the square to La Grande Maison, my brother's residence, and were now entering via the kitchen, as usual. Maëline, her brown curls pulled back in a bouncy ponytail, greeted us with exuberance, her face red and sweaty. The heat in the kitchen was even more unbearable than the ongoing heatwave outside.

'I'm so glad you're here! I have all these things I want you to try. Sit, sit!'

She swept us out of the kitchen and into the much cooler dining room, completely made over from the gloomy room it used to be. The light and airy space now had baby blue walls with painted white flowers, flowy, cream-coloured curtains, and a large, beech table – a far cry from the dark furniture of old. Along one wall, a wide dresser held a myriad of dishes and bowls.

'When did you say you were opening that B&B?' I grinned at my baby brother, who had been opposed to the idea for the longest time but also wanted to please the girl who I was sure would soon be his fiancée.

'First, we'd have to get rid of the swastikas in the basement,' Maëline said as she put yet another dish on the sideboard, her soft voice somehow incongruous with her words.

'They're part of the history of the house,' David countered in a tone that implied this wasn't the first time he'd uttered those words. 'And why would we show our guests into the basement anyway?'

'They might be looking for a broom or something.'

'Then they'd be looking in the wrong place. But' – he held up a finger as Maëline opened her mouth for a retort – 'just in case they do wander into the basement for whatever reason, we can enlighten them and perhaps delight them with a story of the Nazi occupation of Saint-Maurice.'

Maëline shuddered. 'Just what they wanted to hear, I'm sure.'

'Can we just eat? You didn't invite my sister and Beau to try and win them to your side, did you?'

Correction. They must have secretly married twenty years ago. After Maëline glared at David, she pointed at each of the dishes in turn. 'Veal terrine with asparagus, vol-au-vents with crab and asparagus, salad with anchovies, artichoke soup, mini potato gratins, savoury panna cotta with cauliflower and gorgonzola, *jambon à la greque*, prawn bruschetta, lamb carpaccio, and strawberry charlotte. I think they've all survived the heat, but let's not wait till they won't.'

Eyes wide with anticipation, Beau was the first in line. But I waved a confused hand at the buffet.

'Was there supposed to be a party I wasn't invited to?'

'Oh, err, no.' Maëline probably blushed, but with her face already red, that didn't show. 'I'm practising. You know, for when we open.'

Beau, his plate overflowing, sat down and inhaled. 'I think I'll just move in. How much do you charge?'

Maëline and David looked at each other, and I smiled as I filled my plate. All dreams and no plans. My hotel would be safe for now.

'*Coucou!* Sorry we're late.' My mother entered the room, looking not a bit sorry, followed by Benoît Le Roux.

'We're not sorry,' he declared in his booming voice. 'We were kissing.'

Everyone but David enjoyed my brother's pained expression. Even if *Maman* and Benoît had not been making out, it was worth Benoît saying so just to see my brother squirm. I suspected that was the case here, but *Maman*, who never stopped raising us after we left home and instead included everyone else in her admonitions of what she thought needed to be corrected, did not set him straight.

Rubbing his hands together, Benoît joined Maëline at the array of food, while my mother enveloped me in a tight hug.

Then she moved on to Beau, squeezing his arms to his body so he couldn't take the bite he'd been preparing for.

We all ate while my mother chatted, as we always did, and by the time she was ready for food, the rest of us took our time to digest.

David caught my eye. 'Maëline told me not to bring it up, but are you okay?'

Maëline bounced on her chair and David winced, so he would probably have a bruise on his shin by tomorrow. Still, I smiled. For an irritatingly stiff little brother, he was quite sweet. 'I will be, thank you. It's all just a bit much right now.'

'What happened?' He made a swift movement to dodge another kick. 'I mean, you don't have to talk about it if you don't want to.'

I leaned back in my chair, carefully putting my fork down on the edge of the plate so I could think about my answer. I didn't feel like rehashing the same short version I'd given everyone at the hotel. For them, that was all I could manage, but this was my family. They cared about me and not my salacious story.

'So, you know I was supposed to have a party, right?'

David nodded, but Beau interrupted with his mouth full. 'Don't forget about the keys.'

'Right. Well, it's probably unrelated, but...' Beau huffed, but I continued, 'We had promised Céline to help her at the *vide-grenier*, and I thought it would be a good opportunity to get rid of my key collection.'

My mother gasped, then applauded softly. I gave her a small smile.

'Well, people had already bought some of the prettier, framed ones, but I still had the basketful when we were packing up to leave. Then two guys knocked Beau on the head and stole the box that contained the keys. I mean, there were other things in there too, and they could have picked a random box in hopes of a good haul.'

Beau shook his head. 'That's a lot of violence for a very unsure outcome. Even crooks aren't that stupid.'

'But the keys aren't worth anything either. Why are you so sure that's what they were after?'

Keeping his eyes on his plate, Beau shrugged and took another bite.

'Anyway, we spent the hottest part of the day at the police station, but then I had to get back for the party. Oh, I forgot to say, we met a lady at the *vide-grenier* who seemed very nice, so I invited her to the party. To be honest, I didn't think she'd come, with the heat and all, but she showed up with a friend.'

I swallowed, remembering the few short moments I'd spoken to Delphine. I hadn't even had the chance to get to know her before she was gone.

'And then, suddenly, Franck shows up. Just comes to my door, as if it's the most natural thing in the world. Beau went to meet him, but he wouldn't leave, so... I... had to. Talk to him, I mean.'

'She was brilliant.' Beau beamed at me, lifting my spirits. 'Told him straight to his face to f— go away.'

'Can you believe he had the nerve to ask for my help?' I asked the table in general.

'Help *him*?' Benoît was outraged in my stead. His voice rattled the glasses in the dresser. He had only known me a short while, but no doubt my mother had told him the whole story, and he was a very righteous man.

'Help him how?' Maëline asked.

'Do you remember a few weeks ago, when Beau caught that gang leader who then disappeared? Apparently, the police think Franck had something to do with that. He said, since I was so good with murders, could I find out what really happened?'

'And she said, cool as can be, "I don't do missing persons" and slammed the door in his face.' Beau grinned widely, showing a piece of lettuce stuck in his teeth.

My mother clapped again, but David and Benoît looked serious.

'So Franck comes to your door, and then, what, ten minutes later someone's dead?' David asked.

I took a shaky breath. 'Something like that. I don't know exactly when she died. I signed up a few clients, so that took a while, and when I was done, the person we'd met that morning, Capucine, said she couldn't find her friend. When I went out to look for her, there she was.'

'But why her?' Benoît asked. Apparently, he subscribed to Beau's view that it must have been Franck who killed her, as he didn't ask who could have done it.

'That's why I'm not convinced Franck was the murderer,' I said. They all stared at me.

'But... who...?' my mother started.

'Exactly,' Beau agreed.

'I know he seems the obvious suspect, but he didn't know I'd be having a party, and even I didn't know Delphine would be present, nor that she would go out to the courtyard in the middle of a heatwave.'

'So she caught him doing something. Like being where he wasn't supposed to be.' Beau had made up his mind.

'With *one* of my shoes?' I asked but didn't catch the answer as my phone pinged, and I looked at the message.

It was from a withheld number. *Murder weapon in the car with Cyp. They think I did it. Please help me.*

All the blood drained from my head, and I felt dizzy. First my house, now my phone. He was closing in.

'What? What is it?' someone said. Blood pumping in my ears distorted the voice, and the screen I stared at blurred. Someone said my name. But not in the demeaning way I expected. Franck's presence, even just in my phone, made him an almost physical threat in my mind, and I had to convince myself he wasn't right there with me in the room.

There were other people there who cared. I wasn't alone. That certainty brought me out of the spiral of fear that had been sucking me in. My vision cleared, revealing concerned faces around me. When my heartbeat slowed a little, I tried to talk, then coughed to make myself heard. 'It's from Franck. They now suspect him of Cyprien's death too.'

It made no sense. Cyprien was his best friend, his second in command, his right-hand man. He would do anything for Franck. Even kill, as he'd made clear before Franck ever uttered his own threat. Why would Franck kill him?

'Perhaps... I *should* look into it?'

13

Still or sparkling?

'No!'

Though Benoît's voice was the loudest, the answer had come from everyone at the table.

'What you should do is to get as far away from him as possible,' *Maman* said, and they all agreed.

They were right. Of course they were right. I tapped out a reply. *How did you get this number?* Then I blocked his and left it at that.

'I've already removed myself from my own house. I'm staying with Sandrine Lardy for the time being. They're cleaning the house as we speak, but...' I'd called the cleaners from the hotel that morning – Beau did not remember being asked to call – and they said they could start straight away, but even with all trace of yesterday removed, I'd need a mental cleanse to be able to enter my own house without seeing *her* there.

'How nice of her,' *Maman* said. She wasn't keen on Sandrine, and I knew exactly why. Her great idol, Apolline Bailly, had deemed the Lardys 'not their kind of people'. New money and all that. Apolline was very good at forgetting her own money was new when she could claim generations of Baillys living in Saint-Maurice. Unfortunately, *Maman* seemed to have a filter for any dubious thing Apolline did or said.

'We should probably go back to Sandrine's now, actually,' Beau said.

Sipping my water, I studied him. It was not common for him to shy away from people, especially people he liked, and though he considered my brother a bit stuck up – which he was – he normally enjoyed being around my family. I clearly wasn't the only one affected by everything that had happened.

'Good idea,' I agreed, though I could have easily sat here for another hour. Forget about everything and simply chat the time away. But I couldn't do that to the young man who'd been there for me even before he moved in above my studio.

I donned my wide-brimmed sun hat and oversized shades, hugged my family good-bye, and traipsed along beside him on the dusty road back to the hotel, where I'd parked my car. I didn't even consider going back in. Gaëlle had everything well under control, and I couldn't deal with more people asking how I was. Instead, I carefully lowered myself onto the boiling seat of my car and slipped off my heels.

'You know, I'm thinking of going round to Capucine's. See how she's doing. I can drop you off at Sandrine's?'

I'd expected him to want to return, but he surprised me by raising his eyebrows. 'Oh. That's a great idea, actually. I quite liked her, so it'll be good to make sure she's all right.'

I gingerly touched the pedals with my bare feet, but they weren't too hot, so we were soon on our way. Beau was still quiet, so I had the ten minutes or so it took us to get to the big house with 1874 on its roof to worry whether she'd want to see us unannounced. The villa stood on its own, hidden from the road by a hedge, so clearly Capucine wasn't interested in community to begin with, and certainly not after the shock she'd had the day before. But when another elegant woman, this one in her fifties, with silver hair, opened the door, I was taken aback.

'Ah. *Bonjour.* We're looking for Capucine?' Strange plots formed in my head – perhaps Capucine was not who she said she was, and this woman, the real Capucine, would have no idea what we were talking about. The lady pursed her lips and I braced myself.

'Madame Jamin is indisposed. Can I give her a message?'

My imagination screeched to a halt, and I smiled with unfounded relief. 'Can you tell her it's Julie and Thibault? She might want to see us. We were there, yesterday. We'd like to know if she's all right.'

The lady's eyebrows rose almost imperceptibly. 'Wait here.'

She disappeared into the house, leaving us gathering perspiration on the doorstep.

'I thought we had the wrong house for a second,' I confessed.

'Couldn't have been the wrong house. Would have been the wrong lady. But Capucine did say she was going to call a friend.'

The lady returned to the door with a far less haughty air. She smiled and opened the door to let us in. 'Forgive me. After the shock Capucine has had, I don't think she should be dealing with any door-to-door people.'

She led us into an opulently but tastefully decorated room. Both the curtains and the shutters had been closed to keep the sun out, and there were only a few lights on, but below the high ceilings the walls were covered in classical paintings, the way ordinarily only museums show off their collections. There was no TV in the room, or anything that would remind me I wasn't in a bygone age, apart from the electric light and the old-fashioned dumbphone on a small table next to Capucine's seat.

Capucine stood and came towards us, arms outstretched, embracing us both, though she had to stoop slightly to reach me, despite my heels. Then she looked at her friend. 'I'm perfectly fine, Constance. Meet Julie Belmain and Thibault Fouquet. Constance Calin,' she introduced us to her friend.

'That's what you say, and then you shut yourself up in this dark room,' Constance chided.

'I went out this morning, didn't I?'

'And that I could easily have done for you.'

'They were just groceries,' Capucine explained as we chose our seats. Beau picked a large armchair covered in rich-hued pashminas, and I perched on a dainty Louis XVI chair.

'This room is beautiful,' I remarked. 'I don't wonder you wouldn't want to leave it.'

Capucine glanced around the room with affectionate appreciation. 'Thank you. I never had pretty things growing up, so when I married an affluent man, I made sure to surround myself with as many as I could find.'

'Still or sparkling?' Constance asked, holding up two bottles of water.

'I'm so blessed with a friend like Constance,' Capucine said with a smile at her friend. 'I'm sure you two feel the same way.'

I nodded, suddenly unsure what to say, except, 'I'm glad you're feeling all right.'

Capucine sighed, pulling her feet up on the divan where she sat. 'It was a huge shock. I can't say I'm entirely over it, but I'm coping. My biggest issue is the guilt. *I* brought her there. *I* led her to her death. Yes, I know, Constance, I couldn't have known what would happen, but I can't help how I feel. If I hadn't invited her, she would still be alive.'

Great, now I could add guilt to my own list of bad feelings. It was my party Delphine had attended, after all.

'It was her decision to go.' Constance knelt on an oversized cushion on the floor between Beau and Capucine. A candle on a stand behind her lit her silvery hair up like a halo.

'I know, *chérie*, but it's difficult for me to take advice from you, since I know you didn't like her.'

I blinked at the sudden barb and sipped my water, but Capucine seamlessly turned to me, the big, yellow gem on her finger glittering in the light of a Tiffany lamp beside her.

'So, have they arrested Franck Fouquet?'

'Not as far as I know.'

'He's now wanted for two murders,' Beau suddenly said, drawing gasps and hands to throats from the ladies.

'But he couldn't have done that second one,' I hastened to add, not knowing why I felt I had to defend him. No, that wasn't how I felt. I was only setting the record straight. Why did I think I was defending him? 'At least not this morning. He was in the hotel where I could see him all that time. His best friend was found in a burnt-out car,' I explained after a confused headshake from Constance.

Capucine frowned. 'It wouldn't surprise me if he had still done it, somehow.'

'How exactly do you know him?' Beau asked.

Remembering her outburst at the mention of Franck's name yesterday, I prepared myself, and I saw Constance do the same. But Capucine remained quite calm.

'You're his nephew, am I correct?' Beau nodded. 'Do you know of Bandit?' He shook his head. 'That was his company's name. Isn't that audacious? It gets worse. His tagline was "It's a steal". Well, with the low prices he asked for some of the antiques he had on his website, I thought he was right. That is, I thought they were stolen. But when I checked them out, the owners had indeed put the pieces up for sale, so I ordered a few. I waited and waited. Called the number on the website a few times and was told there was a problem in shipping. Then there was a sales tax hold-up. Eventually, the number was disconnected. Then the website went dark.

'It turned out that those items *were* up for sale, just not by him. He'd bamboozled me, and countless others with me. I used the contacts I had through my late husband to track the company to him, but it was no good. I couldn't make my claims stick. For me, it wasn't even so much the money he'd swindled me out of. I'd bought those pieces for a good friend and client of mine, but I now had to renege on my promises, not only to her but to many others. It wrecked my reputation at the time. So you can see why I'm not favourably inclined towards him.'

Ouch. I'd heard the stories from my own clients after Franck targeted my beauty blog, and I knew he'd run other schemes as well, but this was the first time I heard directly from one of those victims. 'Still, it's quite a leap from fraud to murder. What makes you jump to that conclusion?'

'Didn't you do the same? I mean, who else?'

That was the question we kept coming back to. Perhaps it was time I tried to find an answer. 'But why Delphine? Did Franck know her?'

Capucine looked at Constance, who shrugged. 'Not as far as I know.'

'And he couldn't have known she'd be there.'

'But that would go for any killer. Nobody except Capucine knew Delphine would be there, and Capucine herself didn't know until that morning,' Beau said. He'd made himself comfortable in the big chair. All he was missing was a dressing gown and pipe.

'Do you know if Delphine knew anyone else at the party?' I was treading dangerous ground. All the other guests were there at my invitation as potential future clients. If they had known Delphine, they wouldn't be happy to learn I'd implicated them in what could be perceived as a covert accusation.

Capucine and Constance shared a long look. 'She did,' Constance then declared.

Capucine explained, 'Delphine was part of a ladies' club that Constance and I also belong to. One of the other club members was also at your party. A tall woman named Océane?'

I nodded. 'She came with Yolande. Were she and Delphine friends as well?'

Another shared look between the elegant ladies.

'I know I shouldn't speak ill of the dead, but Delphine wasn't very well liked. I don't know how you put up with her, to be honest,' Constance said to Capucine, then explained, 'She was the type of woman to act friendly to your face, but as soon as she had uncovered a bit of dirt, she'd run a smear campaign about you to everyone who she thought could improve her social or financial standing.'

Images of Bella flashed across my mind. I shook my head lightly to get rid of the unwanted connection. 'That could certainly give a person motive. Do you know if she had done something similarly nasty to Océane?'

Constance sat up straight. 'Oh, Océane is not your killer. No, no, she's lovely. I just meant there might be more people with a motive, as you said.'

Thibault caught my eye with something of his old fervour when it came to investigating. In any other case, Océane would probably have been our next witness to question. However, just an hour ago, Beau had joined my family in a resolute discouragement of any sleuthing on my part. Had I not agreed then? Yet here I was, asking questions in spite of that honest determination.

'So what about the shoe? Can you think of anything that would link Delphine with an expensive shoe, or fashion in general?'

Capucine shrugged, and Constance slowly shook her head. This wasn't getting us anywhere. Time to put an end to the investigation before it had properly started.

'Well, I'm sure the police will work it out. I'm glad you're feeling better, Capucine. Again, I'm so sorry things turned out this way.'

She smiled and rose to see us to the door. 'Please don't blame yourself. The fault lies entirely with the killer.'

'As long as you remember that too.' I reached up and hugged her again, then followed Beau to the car.

Seated behind the wheel, I dropped my head back. Somehow, this visit had drained me.

'You still don't believe it was him, do you?' Beau asked.

I closed my eyes. 'I know, I know. *Who else.* But at least now we know there might have been a motive.'

'I thought you weren't going to investigate.'

'I wasn't. I'm not. It's just... there's such a big question mark there. How am I supposed to get over this when I have no answers? I feel like a ghost with unfinished business.'

'It only happened yesterday. You have to give the police a chance to do their job.'

I sighed, then said, 'I'd have a lot more confidence in them if it were Jacqueline leading the investigation.' I opened my eyes and saw him nodding. 'Would you mind driving? I've got a splitting headache.'

He agreed and we switched seats. 'Probably the dry air,' I mumbled, but he didn't answer. The air above the asphalt swirled and wiggled in the heat, and I frowned at some idiot on his *trottinette*, an adult-sized scooter, going the other way. They were useful in town, but who would take them to a country road? As I gazed out over the dry, yellow grass of a meadow, showing patches of arid, golden earth underneath, I felt my eyes close. It was only a ten-minute drive. I might as well...

The car crashed to a halt. The seat belt dug painfully into my sternum when I was thrown forward. Dazed, I opened my eyes. The first thing I saw was my beautiful car's hood, wrinkled and dented against a big, yellow rock.

'Wha...?'

'Are you okay?' Beau asked, pushing my shoulder back against the seat. 'I tried to go slowly, but it still made quite an impact.'

'Huh? Wha?' My brain could only produce caveman sounds. Rubbing my neck, I mentally checked for other sore spots, but I seemed to be in one piece. The same could not be said for my poor little car. 'What did you do?'

'I'm sorry, but the brakes were gone. It was either the rock or the steep slope on the other side.'

'But I just had it checked!'

He gave me a dark look. 'I don't think this was regular wear and tear, Julie.'

My breath stuttered as an iron band closed around my chest. 'What?'

'I think you should call Jacqueline.'

'What?!' My hands started to shake, as well as my lower lip. Franck was trying to kill me. He was really trying to kill me! Scenes of us diving over the edge and tumbling down the hillside played before my eyes, and my breaths came fast and shallow.

The sight of Beau rolling his shoulders and gingerly turning his head made me focus. 'Wait, are you all right?'

He nodded, his own breath heavy.

'But... he wouldn't kill you just to get to me. Would he?'

Beau didn't answer. Like a leaf in the wind, my fear flipped to anger. 'But that's crazy! He's actually gone mad!'

'Now do you believe he killed Delphine?' Beau said it softly, but the words hit hard.

Some of the anger made way for more fear. I waited for my heart rate to go down, then, with trembling fingers, called Jacqueline.

14

This is serious!

'Ariëlle.' That was all the greeting Thibault could manage seeing the person on his phone screen after all that time.

The voice of the young woman on the other end was as mocking as it had always been. 'Hello, big brother. I was wondering when you'd call. Still alive, then?'

'So you know.' They had barely made it back to Sandrine Lardy's house before Beau retreated to his room and finally made the call.

She smiled radiantly. 'I always know.'

'Did he know I was going to be in that car? Does he even care?' Though rage boiled in his veins, he kept as calm as he could.

Ariëlle shrugged lightly, her blonde hair falling over her shoulders. 'It's *because* you'd be in that car. She would have panicked. You know how to handle a situation like that. It's scare tactics, Bobo, not murder.'

'Are you sure about that?'

The pretty face on the screen finally turned serious. 'It wasn't him. Can't have been. He's not a murderer.'

'Things aren't always a certain way just because you want them to be so.'

'Ha!' The light-heartedness was back in her voice. 'Then I'll make 'em so.'

'You cannot change what has already happened. And contrary to what you believe, people don't always do what you think or want them to do.' Wasn't that just what had driven them apart from a very young age?

'You'd be surprised.' She laughed.

He swore. 'Ariëlle, this is serious! I could have been killed!'

'But you survived. Obviously.'

'I'm going to tell her.' It was his trump, but also his last resort. He didn't actually mean to tell Julie everything, but if his sister didn't even care about him nearly dying, then maybe she'd pay attention to his threat.

She did. Ariëlle shot up and frowned at the screen. 'You can't! You know that's the most dangerous thing you could do. Not only for her, but for us. For me.'

'We need to meet.' He narrowed his eyes at a framed picture in the background. 'You're home.' She hadn't appeared at his parent's house in years. He'd started to wonder whether she'd even be welcome there any more.

'Come give me a hug?'

'More like a Judas kiss.'

Her laugh tinkled. 'You're right, we do need to talk. Meet me at the old oak tree in an hour?'

Beau hung up without saying goodbye. His own sister didn't care if he lived or died. But then, she had never cared. All she'd ever cared about was herself. He'd once asked her what side she was actually on. 'The winning side, always,' she'd answered. Soon after, she'd chosen to go to an *internat*, a boarding school where she knew the daughter of an influential man in Lyon's underworld would also be attending. She was thirteen at the time.

Ariëlle had always known she was meant for great things. Their mother, concerned for their wellbeing, had tried to steer her and Beau in a more above-board direction, but Ariëlle idolised their dad. She thought she could expand his reach by befriending this other girl. The two did become friends, but gradually, Ariëlle had let go of her own family in favour of her friend's. This was why she hadn't been home in years. Now nineteen, apparently she'd had a reason to change that.

Sneaking out of the Lardys' villa was easy. He passed Natalya, who was outside in the shade with a vape pen. She saw him but looked right through him. Julie's car had been taken to the garage, and without an immediate replacement ready, he had to walk back to the house in order to take his Harley. From the villa, that was a stiff walk, especially since the sun, though no longer at its strongest, was still making itself felt. He did have plenty of time, though, so perhaps he could make a little detour into the bakery.

Seeing Céline would be the perfect balm for his wounds. Neither he nor Julie had sustained any injuries from the crash, save for a few bruises, but hearing his sister talk so carelessly about playing with his life had hurt his pride. She'd probably meant it as a compliment. *You know how to handle a situation like that.* He wished he didn't. Going far away and starting over looked more enticing by the minute.

Except... He wiped the sweat from his forehead when he saw the bakery at the end of the street. He'd have to make that decision soon. And if he did go to LA, he might never see her again. With his new contacts, he had a good shot at a career in film, but by the time it would be established, she would have moved on. Found someone else. His stomach clenched at the thought.

The little bell above the door tinkled when he entered. In his mind, the sound echoed through a dark, lonely space. The bakery was deserted. Then, there was movement in the little corridor, and all darkness lifted. His eclair. He'd never have enough of her.

Wiping his hands on the apron spanning his belly, Monsieur Plaisant, the baker, appeared with a big smile on his face. 'You don't look happy to see me. I'm hurt.' He wasn't hurt.

Monsieur Plaisant had practically seen Beau grow up alongside his daughter, and Beau always had the feeling the baker knew exactly what was going on. Whether he was on Beau's side, though, Beau had never been able to figure out. 'She's out on delivery. I expect she'll be back in thirty minutes or so.'

Beau nodded and left. He'd have to make do without his little pick-me-up. Trudging through the heat, Beau wiped his face again, fanning himself with his hat. The road between the centre of the village and Julie's house seemed twice as long, but at least there'd be water in the fridge once he got there.

Would he miss this place? Probably not. It was a stepping stone, no more. Julie had been a good boss, and he'd had some fun with her sleuthing, but this was not where he wanted to be. Perhaps it was for the best Céline had wanted to be 'just friends'. What if she did want to stay? He couldn't possibly live the rest of his life in this dull old village where everything was the same day in and day out. Well, apart from the murders.

He entered the house and gulped down an entire bottle of water, ignoring his stomach's protest. Then he took a deep breath and braced himself as he opened the door to the courtyard. Seeing the spot where they'd found Delphine again would be difficult, but he'd have to face it sooner or later. Even if he didn't live here much longer, it would be better if he steeled himself for whatever bad things life threw at him.

Strangely, though, the porch looked like it always had. He stood in the shade looking down onto the patio floor and the wall of Julie's house, but the expected image of Delphine lying there did not surface. As soon as he turned his gaze towards the garden, there she was, but she disappeared when he turned back to the spot where she'd died. There were only the wall, the wooden gate, and the gravel of the courtyard. Now he had a new problem, as he was loath to turn away from that spot.

Still, he couldn't stand there, staring at a wall until the end of time. Gritting his teeth, he focused on the shed where he stored his bike. Time would at least be on his side, right? If he survived long enough, the image would fade, and with it the memories of Saint-Maurice and its inhabitants.

First, though, he had to deal with his present predicament: a family that seemed to want him dead. Beau had suspected his sister would turn up again when Uncle Franck was released. As her adoration of their father faded, Ariëlle seemed to have found a new respect for Uncle Franck. Unlike the rest of the family, who considered being caught and going to prison a mark of stupidity, Ariëlle had remained neutral during his trial – and had been his most loyal contact ever since.

Beau had only volunteered to help Uncle Franck because it would give him an opportunity to get away from a family that didn't value him and to be close to Céline, but Ariëlle was immediately on Franck's side. Whether that was out of loyalty or for another reason would only come to light if Ariëlle deemed it necessary.

When he pulled up to the old oak tree in a park just north of the Fouquets' residence, Ariëlle was already there. She came towards him with her arms outstretched and hugged him. He mechanically answered the embrace but didn't feel any warmth towards his sister.

'Oh, Thibault, really? I haven't seen you in over five years, and you're sour about a little accident?'

'I could have died.' He barely restrained his voice, but she would know he was still livid.

'No, you couldn't. It's you! I have every bit of faith in you.' She waved away his anger as if all she'd done was take the last biscuit, and sat on the wide swing hanging off one of the old tree's branches. 'Phew. It's a scorcher, isn't it?'

'Get to the point, Ariëlle. Why does he want to scare her if she's already got rid of all the keys? He told me yesterday, before Julie came to the door, that he didn't need me any more. What's he planning? Did he kill that woman?'

That question sobered Ariëlle, as it had done before. 'I told you, that wasn't him.'

'How are you so sure? Was it you?'

She shot up, the seat of the swing flying backwards. 'How dare you?!' The swing hit her calves on its way down, but she didn't notice. 'We take what we can take, but we never take a human life. You know that!'

'Do I? It's what we've been taught, but a lot has changed since we were little. You left, so you may not know everything that happened, but after Uncle Franck was caught, Dad got bitter.'

She huffed a laugh. 'That, I know.'

Beau paused. He'd never given a thought to the fact that there must have been something specific that made Ariëlle change allegiances. 'A lot of the guys were dissatisfied with the strict rules he imposed afterwards. Hence why Seive had such an easy go of his bid for power.'

Ariëlle huffed again, but the sneer on her face contained no humour. 'You think that was Seive? Shows what you know.'

Beau winced internally. That was low. He knew Ariëlle had always been the favourite. But after he had put an end to the rebellion a few weeks ago, he'd thought he'd won some favour. Now she was telling him Seive had been no more than a puppet? Had everybody else known? They couldn't have done, or the rebellion would still be going. Some of the key figures had left for Lyon or Paris, but most of the guys had come back with their tails between their legs.

'Franck?'

She clicked her tongue, flicking her long, blonde hair over her shoulder. 'You've guessed it.'

Beau took a deep breath. Of course it was Franck. Never openly, as per family values, but in the shadows, pulling the strings. Trying to take over the organisation from his own brother. And in a way, Beau had even helped him. By taking Seive out of the picture and thereby quelling the mutiny, Beau had paved the way for Franck to get closer to Patrick again.

But within all those machinations, neither scaring Julie nor killing a random woman seemed to fit in. Whatever Franck was up to – and Beau was convinced Franck's next plan had already been set in motion – it was not going to end well for Julie if he were to succeed. Franck wanted money and power. He always had. It was obvious that he now also wanted revenge on Julie. But there was something else going on. Something Beau couldn't put his finger on. And that scared him most of all.

'So whose side are you on?' he asked Ariëlle, just to see if she would confirm what he already knew.

She gave him a cold smile. 'As always, the winning side.'

'Your moral compass is broken. It's forever spinning round.'

She grinned a little more loosely then and sat back down on the swing. 'See, that's where you're wrong. It always points to the same thing. That may just not be your moral north.'

Shaking his head, he decided to leave that wherever it was. 'So where is Seive?'

Uncharacteristically, Ariëlle bowed her head and stared at her feet. Beau narrowed his eyes. Had he finally found something that she cared about? But if Seive was no more than a pawn, it couldn't be him. Also, he was old. And ugly. Why would she care about *him*? No, whatever it was Ariëlle was unsure about, it would not be an alliance with Michel Seive.

'Nobody knows,' she said to the ground. Then she took a deep breath and looked him in the eye. 'I need your help.'

15

Get over your fear and think

'Okay, you need to get a grip.'

I blinked through my tears at the ex-policewoman I thought was my friend. Jacqueline had a very low tolerance for self-pity, but I was pretty sure an attempt on my life did not count as self-pity. She'd rushed over to Sandrine's villa as soon as I let her know we were back. Sandrine had been shocked to hear of our accident and offered us anything we could possibly need, but both Beau and I had wanted to be alone for a while and retreated to our rooms. When Jacqueline arrived, I'd sat up, and she'd joined me on the bed.

'No, I know you're distraught, and I agree, this is serious.' Jacqueline squeezed my hand to underline her words. 'But we need evidence. Someone' – even if she agreed Franck was the most likely person, she purposely left out his name – 'is playing a dangerous game, but right now, you have no proof that the murder at your house, the disabling of your car brakes, and the violent death of your ex-husband's best friend are connected.'

'How can you say that? Of course they are connected! *I'm* the connection, if nothing else. Why would anyone cut my brake lines if not in connection with one or even both of those murders?'

'Obviously. But what I said was, we need evidence. Apart from the fact that you're Franck's alibi, you shouldn't have anything to do with the death of his best friend, so does that mean you are 'connected' enough for the attempt on your life to be linked to it? Delphine was killed with your shoe in your house, but why would anyone want to kill you afterwards, unless you were the intended victim all along?'

I whimpered. Not only had that thought been going round and round in my head ever since I'd called Jacqueline from the car, but in the meantime, I'd developed an unhealthy dose of guilt because not only had Delphine died at *my* party, but she also might have been a senseless victim of the death that should have been mine.

'So, you need to get a grip and focus.' Another squeeze of my hand. 'You need to think logically, so stop letting your fear control your thoughts.'

'That's easy for you to say.' I sniffed.

'No. It's not.'

My lip quivered again when I looked in her eyes. The same warm eyes that had helped me through the horrendous time after I'd left Franck's influence and was trying to get him convicted. If not for abuse, then at least for fraud. That's what he was eventually convicted for. Jacqueline and my mother had almost had to carry me to the courtroom, I was so scared. Gradually, though, I had worked myself out of the hold he had on me.

But that fear was back with a vengeance. I wished I could crawl under the covers and wait till it was all over. Before they locked him away, Franck had said, 'Enjoy life, *mon amour*. In four years, it'll be over.' During those four years, the power of his words had faded. My fear had flared up a few months ago, when he was released, but nothing had happened, and I had settled down again. Until now.

What was he planning? Was he really going to kill me? But then why kill the wrong person? Delphine and I looked nothing alike, and this man had been married to me. He wouldn't have mistaken her for me. And the brakes were a strange roundabout way for him to kill me too. For one, it could have made for more innocent deaths than just mine. Had Franck lost all humanity in prison?

'I know you think Franck wants to kill you. And I'm not saying it's not him. But he came to ask you for help. I mean... the killer snuck into your house. They could just as easily have done that at night and murdered you in your sleep.'

I gasped, bunching the bed covers up beside me. Was this supposed to make me feel better?

'I'm only saying, why make it difficult? What if whoever murdered Delphine did so because they wanted Delphine dead?'

I shook my head. 'But nobody knew she'd be there.'

'Except the people already at the party.'

'Yes, but then why use my shoe? They'd have had to go into my house to get it, and none of my clients ever visit the house.'

Jacqueline squared her shoulders. 'Look, I don't know. But that's what I mean. You're the person most likely to have all the clues, even if you don't yet know what they are. You've done this before, Julie. You need to get over your fear and think.'

'But none of it makes sense!' I exclaimed, my eyes watering again.

'If anyone can figure it out, you can. I've already contacted the few friends I have left at the *bureau*, and they'll let me know if anything useful comes up. But from what I gather, they're just as stumped as we are. "Random intruder" was the term used.'

If my shoulders could sag any more, they would. 'Actually, that would almost make the most sense right now. Except it doesn't explain why my car is currently at the garage.'

Jacqueline took a deep breath, savoured it for a second, then blew it out again. 'So what do you usually do when you solve a murder? Make a list of suspects? Question witnesses?'

I frowned, surprised by the question, but then smiled in spite of the situation. 'You make me sound like a professional. I just happened to know the right people and ask the right questions. But I can't walk up to Franck and work out his motives from small talk about his hobbies.'

Jacqueline's eyebrows shot up. '*That's* how you did it?'

'No! Well, a bit. Maybe? I don't even know! I just chat to the people involved and they tell me random things that gradually start to make sense. How's that for professional?' I paused. 'Also, I usually had Beau there with me to ask any awkward questions. I don't think he'll be first in line to question his family. He was in that car too. In fact, I probably owe him my life now. He'll be rubbing that in once we get through this. *If* we survive.'

'We will.' Thibault came barging in, looking a whole lot more stable than when he'd gone upstairs.

'How are you so sure?' I asked, secretly a bit jealous of his confidence.

'Think about it: if he wanted to kill you, he would have done it already.'

Jacqueline nodded at his words, but they only annoyed me. 'Thanks. That makes me feel so much better. But what about the brake lines?'

'They were cut while we were in the valley. Going up, we were bound to go more slowly, and so there was less chance of us actually getting hurt.'

My mouth went slack. 'But then... why?'

'To scare us? Like when he stole your box of keys. You know that was him. No other reason than to unsettle you. But you didn't listen, so he had to go further.'

'But... why?' I glanced between Beau and Jacqueline. 'Scare us into doing what? Or out of what?'

Jacqueline pursed her lips. 'If it was Franck, he did ask you to help, and you refused.'

'So killing another woman and cutting the brake lines is going to make me want to *help* him?'

Beau put up a hand. 'I only meant the brakes. That makes sense as a scare tactic. The murder still makes no sense to me.'

'So you think they're unrelated.'

He only shrugged.

Slowly nodding, I gestured for Beau to sit, and he rounded the bed and belly-flopped onto the other side, making Jacqueline and me bounce.

'You're pretty sure of this,' I stated, as he seemed his old self despite what we'd been through. Something had changed between the moment we arrived at Sandrine's and now. What had he been up to?

'It fits Franck's character.'

That was true. Manipulation was his forte. 'Jacqueline thinks we should solve the case.'

He looked up, one corner of his mouth pulled up.

'Which I think means helping Franck...'

Beau's gaze fell to the bed covers, but then he sat up. 'We need a list. I'll grab my pad.'

He left the room, and Jacqueline grinned. 'Aha! You do make a list.'

Seeing both my friends eager to help me lifted my spirits, if only a little. 'I think we'll need several. Even if Beau is right and we can discount the brakes, we still have two murders and a disappearance that could all be linked, *or* might not be at all. But we'll have to gather all the facts and separate them before we can make any sense of the situation.'

Beau returned to the room, flicking through his sketch-book to find an empty page.

'We'll start with Seive.' I lifted my chin to show myself I was ready, willing, and able. 'What do we know?'

'He killed his wife with a statue.' Beau was still proud of the fact that he'd worked that out.

I suppressed a smile. 'Yes, and you got him arrested for that.'

'Not quite,' Jacqueline said. 'Examination of the statue later proved that it was the murder weapon, but at the time of Seive's disappearance, he was only wanted for questioning.'

'So he probably saw what was coming and found a safe place to lie low,' I concluded.

'Kind of. Except he didn't. You know that *domaine* near Pruniers, the one with the clock?'

'Oh, yes, we went there with Ben Hjerson for a garden show. You mean the clock with the second hand, right?' I asked. Only a few weeks ago, I'd visited the wine estate with one of Hollywood's biggest names and pointed out the antique tower clock's famous feature.

Jacqueline nodded. 'They were struggling financially. That's why they said yes to all those kinds of events – garden shows, wedding photos, that sort of thing – but in the end they had to sell. Guess who bought it?'

Beau wiggled his head. 'Michel Seive. But we were there around the same time he disappeared. Had it already changed owners then?'

'It hadn't. Michel still had the papers to sign. Which he did. A week after his disappearance. Of course, I'd been kicked off the force by then, but—'

'You left with your head held high,' Beau interrupted.

Jacqueline smirked, but I could tell she was pleased with his compliment. 'Like I said, I still have some feelers out at the *bureau*. Apparently, Seive showed up out of the blue, and since the owners still desperately wanted to sell, they drummed up a notary and got the deal sealed.'

'Wouldn't they have frozen all his assets?' I asked.

Both Jacqueline and Beau laughed. 'That's cute, that you think we'd be able to get to all his "assets",' Jacqueline teased. 'Of course, they tried keeping an eye on the estate, but Seive didn't return. What did happen, was that the famous second hand was stolen from the clock.'

Beau scribbled in his sketchbook, but I frowned. 'Do they know who stole it?'

'Nope. And nobody knew why. The second hand on its own isn't worth anything. Just a decorative piece of wrought iron. Until yesterday, when it turned up again. And in a very interesting place.'

I had the feeling this interesting place was not going to make me especially happy.

Beau did not have that feeling. 'Where?'

'In Cyprien Gréban's burnt-out car. The wounds on the body, as far as could be determined, seem to be consistent with that second hand being used to knock him over the head. I say "seem to be". Both the car and the body were burnt to a crisp. I mean, it was an exceptionally hot fire. There wasn't much the *techniciens* could learn from the remains.'

I drummed my fingers on the bed. 'So there's a definite link between Seive's disappearance and Cyprien's murder.'

'And both of them were Franck's seconds. As in second-in-command,' Beau explained when I frowned at him.

'Seive was working for Franck?' He gave me a knowing look that I didn't want to explore. All right, Seive worked for Franck. I did not need to know how Beau knew this. 'You think the choice of weapon was symbolic?'

He widened his eyes. 'Obviously. Seive got too big for his breeches. The message is clear: he should have stayed a second.'

'But it was Cyprien in that car,' Jacqueline said.

Beau's face fell. 'Maybe he joined up with Seive?'

'Never.' I shook my head so violently, my ponytail swished against my cheek. 'That man lived and breathed Franck Fouquet. You would sooner join the police than Cyprien would go against Franck.'

'So who would want Franck's right-hand man out of the way?' Jacqueline asked. 'What's the symbolism there?'

'Or...' Beau paused for effect, or perhaps to put words to his thought, 'Seive took the thing himself, and he killed Cyprien in order to be the only second?'

Jacqueline and I both raised an eyebrow at him.

'One second killing the other with a second hand that he owned himself?' Jacqueline mocked. 'Just a little far-fetched, don't you think? Why not just go for the boss and take his place? That was what he was trying for with your father, wasn't it? And he did that on Franck's orders, so why bother with the other helper?'

'Just a thought.' Beau shrugged. 'I still think it's suspicious that Franck chose so obvious a spot to be seen right around the time someone "matching his description" carried out the murder of *his* best friend.'

I sighed. 'Looks like we have more questions than answers already. And how are we supposed to find more evidence about either of these cases? Our only link to that world has left it.' I glanced pointedly at Thibault, who recoiled. Again, that nagging feeling surfaced that he knew more than he let on.

'They don't even take me seriously. If I show up now, asking questions, whoever is doing all these killings will have me hanging off a butcher's hook in no time.' He hesitated. 'I mean, maybe I could ask Constantin.'

'Apolline's son? What would he know?' Despite Apolline's obsession with social standing, she'd not been able to control her son's proclivity for crime. He'd spent a few years in Paris after school but had been spotted in and around Saint-Maurice for about a month or so. I'd seen Beau talk to him on more than one occasion.

'He's been trying to slime his way into my family.'

'Oh. I thought he was your friend.'

'Friend, friend... If my friends were kitchen staff, then Gío would be my sous-chef and Constantin would be the one cleaning the deep fat fryer. But he may have made other connections than me by now. Which could also mean he would want to avoid me, but I can try.'

Jacqueline nodded. 'All right, that will be your task. And I will put a bit more pressure on my ex-colleagues to see if they can give me any more. It'll be the last time they'll have to deal with me, anyway.'

I gave her a half-hearted smile. Though I appreciated her efforts, I couldn't help but feel she might be gone before we'd made a dent in this investigation. My boyfriend might be coming back, but now I'd have another friend in America, only to be reached digitally. I'd miss her terribly.

'Let's hope you can both find out some more, because we haven't got very far yet. Then there's only Delphine's... case left.' I swallowed. As much as I tried to take Jacqueline's advice and think logically, I still couldn't get rid of the personal feeling of loss when it came to Delphine. 'Beau is convinced Franck is her killer. You and I aren't sure, but we have no alternatives. I think we need to take a leaf out of Sherlock Holmes's book and start eliminating the impossible. So, who was there?'

Beau summed up as he wrote. 'You and I, of course, but we don't count. Do I need to put Marie and Nienke on here?'

'No, start with Capucine, then add Yolande, Océane, and the other friend, what was her name?'

'Anne-Colombe. You want to put Capucine on the suspect list?'

'This is just a list of people at the party. Then there's Chantelle and her friend Lela.'

Beau made a face. 'She's definitely suspicious.'

'Only because you think she's after your job.'

'She is! Did you see her cooing over the equipment, and your style, and how she'd love to work with you? She actually said that!'

I had to bite my lip to keep from laughing. He might be planning to leave, but he still had some pride in his work. 'So? Perhaps I could have two assistants. I think you'd work together well.'

Beau opened his mouth for a retort, but Jacqueline was faster. 'Can we get back to finding a killer, please?' She blew out some air. 'It's a wonder you two got anywhere before. Who else is on the list?'

'Agathe and her friend.'

'Maxine.' Beau noted them both down.

'And then Sandrine and those blondes.'

'Natalya and Astrid. So that makes eleven. If we count the last three.'

Jacqueline lifted her chin. 'We should. But we should also add your friends, Julie. Just because you know a person, doesn't mean they can't be bad.'

I wrinkled my nose at her. 'And just because you're still a policewoman at heart, doesn't mean everyone is a killer.'

'So, thirteen?' Beau asked. I stuck my tongue out at him, but he continued, 'That's a lot. Is there anyone we can discount?'

'Yes. My friends.'

'Hey, I'm only doing this because you won't believe it was Franck.'

'You know how the sidekick always suspects the wrong person?'

'Oh, I see, I'm *your* sidekick.'

'You are literally my assistant.'

'So was Passepartout in *Around the World in Eighty Days*, and he was definitely the hero, saving the princess and all.'

'Look at you and your literary references.'

'*Arrête!*' Jacqueline suddenly exclaimed and jumped off the bed. 'If all you two can do is bicker, I'm out of here.'

I felt like a toddler being admonished. 'No, please stay. I'm sorry. We're sorry. Aren't we?' I glared at Beau, conveniently blaming him.

'As the assistant-hero, I can only apologise.'

Was that an apology, or a continuation of the argument? I kept glaring, but Jacqueline looked at her phone.

'Okay, well, I can't add anything useful to the party talk, and Ken and I have dinner reservations. I mean, I'm happy to stay if you need me.'

She raised her eyebrows at me, but I didn't want to ruin her romantic date, so I shook my head. 'No, I'm fine now. Thank you so much, Jacquie, truly.'

She leaned down and hugged me tightly. 'You'll get through this as you have done before. You're a strong woman, remember?'

'And I don't need men.' I grinned at Beau. 'Well… sometimes.'

He still wasn't over my calling him a sidekick. 'I was going to say, I'll tell Léon.'

Jacqueline laughed on her way to the door. 'He knows. Stay strong, and I'll see you tomorrow.'

She waved and closed the door behind her, leaving me with a grumpy Thibault.

Letting myself fall back onto the bed, I sighed loudly. 'I hate this.'

We were both quiet for a minute or so. In spite of our silly bickering, I was happy to have Beau there. We'd been through a lot together. And now, he was the only one who knew how I felt.

'I keep seeing her there,' I finally admitted. 'What if that never stops? How can I go back to my own house?'

Speaking my fears brought yet more tears to my eyes. I hated that I had a more emotional reaction to the idea of not being able to return home than to the life lost in it. It felt selfish to worry more about a place than about Delphine's family and friends losing a loved one, but since this was where her death touched my life, I supposed it was only natural. Still, my intellectual reasoning did nothing for the guilt I felt.

'I went back,' Beau said after a pause.

I wiped my eyes and sat up to look at him.

'I wanted my bike, and I hoped that if I saw the place in my mind for real, it might help.'

When no more came, I asked, 'Did it?'

He frowned at the bedding. 'I'm not sure.'

I lowered myself back down. 'Maybe I should go see the place too. I can't stay with Sandrine forever. According to Jacqueline, she could even be a killer.' What would be worse, sleeping at the scene of a crime, or sleeping under one roof with a murderer? Of course, I'd already done that before. So had Sandrine.

I pressed my wrist to my forehead, then got up. 'We do need to know what happened. We'll never put this behind us if we don't. But it's all such a jumble.'

Beau looked up and nodded. 'We're not the only ones working on this. Chagrin may be an idiot, but I have faith in Rouletabille. And even if he doesn't work it out, I'm sure you will. In time.'

His words heartened me. I would figure it out. Not just for me, but also for him. 'But not right now. I'm hungry and

I need a change of scenery. I'm going to the hotel. Are you coming?'

16

And now we're getting married

Happy to have Beau on my side again, I stepped into the corridor with a smile. 'Oh, hello.'

Sebastian Tombs was at the top of the stairs, just inside the corridor on our side of the villa. He was holding up two bottles of wine and studying them, but when I greeted him, he quickly put down one of the bottles on a side table and turned to smile at me in a most disarming manner that made all my alarm bells ring. What was it with these house guests? Ronan didn't know his Grand Crus from his Villages, and Sebastian just happened to be outside my room after we'd been discussing a murder there.

'They say the weather is finally going to turn,' Sebastian offered.

'It'd better,' Beau answered behind me.

They entered into a conversation about the heat that gave me time to let Sandrine know we wouldn't be there for dinner. I found our hostess in the living room, chatting softly with

Lips, err... Astrid. When I entered, Sandrine stretched out her hand towards me.

'Like Julie, for instance.'

I raised my eyebrows with a curious smile.

'I was just telling Astrid that it doesn't matter how humble your origins are. If you want to, you can make something of yourself.'

Though I wouldn't say my origins were exactly humble, I stood behind the sentiment. Sure, I had the safety net of a rich family, but I'd built my own business from the ground up. 'Absolutely, you go for it.'

I was going to leave it at that and had already turned to Sandrine to inform her of my dinner plans, but Astrid gave me a wide-eyed smile and latched on.

'That's so sweet of you,' she said with a slight accent. Her demeanour now was a night-and-day difference from what it had been earlier at my party. Remembering how she'd tried to mimic the vicomtesse the night before, I wondered if this change could be a reflection of how different Sandrine herself was in her own home. 'Everyone has been so kind. Anne-Colombe said the same thing yesterday. Something about finding my way to happiness whichever path I took. I think. She spoke rather quickly.'

My ears pricked up. 'You spoke to Anne-Colombe at the party?'

She nodded happily. 'I was afraid the event would be terribly posh, but then I saw your pictures and I realised it couldn't possibly be.'

I ignored the slight as it wasn't meant that way. Probably.

'I said something like that to the person nearest me, and she laughed. Said even posh people like to do silly things sometimes.'

Once more, I ignored the slight but intended to say something if she did it again.

'That was Anne-Colombe. She said her friend Océane was the poshest person she knew, but she was sure Océane would book a session before the party was over.'

I nodded. 'She did. Only I didn't realise she was so posh, as you put it.'

'Oh, yes!' Astrid placed her hands on her knees, almost pushing her bosom out of the slip of a dress she wore. 'Anne-Colombe told me all about her. Apparently, she's related to one of your Kings, probably a Louis.'

That kind of relation must be almost as distant as my own family's relation to the English court. Still, it held value for some of the members of my family, as it must do for Océane's. I gave a smile that I hoped would suffice as an answer.

'I'm meeting her in the village for dinner, actually. Anne-Colombe, I mean.'

'Oh, that reminds me.' I turned to Sandrine. 'Thibault and I were thinking of going into the village for dinner too. Will that inconvenience your cook?'

She smiled. 'Don't worry about that. In this heat, we only eat light things anyway. I'm sure she won't mind at all.'

'Good, thank you.'

'Do you need to borrow my car, since yours is in the valley?'

Oh. I hadn't considered that. I supposed I could get on the back of Beau's bike again, but once was quite enough, if I was honest.

'Anne-Colombe is picking me up in about ten minutes. I'm sure she won't mind taking you as well,' Astrid said.

Thanking her, I asked what it was she was aspiring to achieve. She cast down her gaze and rubbed her upper arm. 'I'm not sure, actually. To be anything but what I was before, really. But I don't have any great talents, like acting or photography.'

This humble side to the beautiful blonde surprised me. Of course, it could all be an act, even though she'd just said she couldn't act. Then I admonished myself. Just because I had some untrustworthy people in my vicinity didn't mean I couldn't trust anyone. Perhaps all this young woman needed was a little push from me. Whatever it was she'd been before and didn't want to be any more, there was bound to be something I could do. She could easily be a model, and I half expected her to own up to that when I said, 'Most of what I do requires skill more than talent, and skill is something you can learn. Don't you have a dream job? Or even just a direction you think you'd like to go in?'

Her eyes started to sparkle, and I knew I'd hit on something.

'Well... yesterday, when I met the vicomtesse... I mean... But that's, like, way out of my league.'

'What, owning a castle? I'd say that is out of pretty much everyone's league.'

Sandrine laughed at my joke, but I secretly admired Astrid for dreaming big.

'Oh, no!' Astrid giggled. 'I only meant I'd love to work for someone sophisticated like her. Be a hostess or something. But I'd have so much to learn!'

Sandrine and I looked at each other. She was just as amused and perhaps slightly endeared by Astrid's unassuming frankness.

'Knowing Hélène,' Sandrine said, 'you're as good as hired. I'll put in a word for you.'

Astrid's breath caught just as the doorbell rang.

'That'll be Anne-Colombe.' I got up to fetch Beau. Astrid followed me, floating on air.

As she went to open the door, I called up the stairs to Beau, who came down immediately.

'Made a new friend?'

He laughed. 'Hardly. I like him, but he and I have nothing in common except a love of drawing. We were discussing the sketch at the top of the stairs.'

We greeted Anne-Colombe and thanked her for the lift, so I couldn't comment on his remark. Personally, I wondered what Sebastian Tombs had been doing in an empty corridor that led nowhere apart from our bedrooms, Beau's and mine. But again I had to ask myself, was I now suspecting everyone because of the few shady characters in my life? Surely not everyone was out to end my life!

'Not a bit of a problem, happy to help,' Anne-Colombe said over her shoulder. 'Astrid told me you had quite a scare.'

I told her about the accident but downplayed how frightened I'd been. Jacqueline had advised me not to tell anyone the cause of the crash but to keep an eye out for slips of the tongue or overly curious questions.

Anne-Colombe, however, did not seem interested. 'That's the second stressful situation in two days. I feel for you, Julie. Did you get enough sleep? I know Capucine didn't, poor thing. Saw her driving out of Villefranche this morning, just as the sun was coming up. Every month, some of my friends get together to do a sun-greeting, that's why I was already out and about. It's a lot of fun to welcome our glorious sun to a new day but easier to do in winter.' She laughed, and I joined in politely, but after she'd parked on the square, I tapped Beau on his arm so he wouldn't go straight into the hotel.

'Why do you think she lied about that?'

Frowning because I was keeping him from his food, he asked flatly, 'Who lied about what?'

'Anne-Colombe. She said she saw Capucine coming out of town as the sun came up, but we were on that road yesterday at the same time, and I couldn't see a thing with the sun in my eyes.'

Beau shrugged, already on his way inside. 'So she made a mistake. She was only making conversation.'

I pursed my lips. Perhaps she was. I was probably just seeing ghosts after all that had happened. I closed my eyes, took a deep breath, told myself I *could* trust people, and forgot all about Anne-Colombe when I smelled the air inside the hotel's restaurant. It was... familiar, somehow. We chose a table, and I searched around for Jeanette, who was at her usual spot in between the restaurant and lounge area so she could oversee both. The radiant smile on her face told me Théo must be better, which explained the familiar scent of the food.

Jeanette caught my gaze and came over to our table.

'Julie, can you believe it? He wasn't really sick. I thought he was, and I was really worried, but then he said he wasn't but that he just couldn't do it any more. And then he said he loved me, and that just made me so happy, and now we're getting married!'

Thibault's laugh rolled around the restaurant, and several people looked our way. 'Well, finally!'

Jeanette's eyes widened, but nothing could disturb her bliss. She absentmindedly accepted my happy hug and congratulations and floated back to her corner, not even taking our orders.

Beau grinned at me. 'He took his sweet time.'

'You're one to talk.' I regretted my words when I saw his reaction, but he otherwise chose to ignore me.

'I'm going to congratulate him. I'll be back with our food.'

He left without asking me what I wanted, but I'd be fine. Théo knew what I liked, and happy Théo would make it extra special. I glanced over at Jeanette, who didn't seem to see anything, staring into the middle distance as she was, sighing every so often. Her happiness rubbed off on me, and I found myself smiling too.

For the first time in two days, some of the tension left my body. I took a deep breath and enjoyed the feeling of being surrounded by familiar faces who were dear to me. I'd spotted Tiana and Lucas in a secluded corner, engrossed in some sort of game with cards. My mother and Benoît were having a formal dinner with two men, probably some political connections. A child I recognised because his mother always smiled at me whined to his father, 'I need to go *pipilette*.'

Madame Dufaux was seated at a table close by with a friend. She held up a spoon. 'Jean doesn't understand the difference between breakfast plates and dinner plates, though they're obviously different sizes. And he puts the cooking cutlery with the tableware. One spoon has a square end, and one is round. He'd see the difference if you asked him, but to him, they're both spoon-shaped.' Madame was the queen of petty complaints, but as long as they were about the husband she so obviously adored, we all took her grievances with a grain of salt.

However, at another table behind me, I could also hear the nasal voice of Isabelle Cochon, the butcher's wife. 'If you want to know whether you've still got it, try out the old folks' home. If the biddies all sit up a little straighter, you've still got it.'

I frowned at this curious statement. All right, *most* of the familiar faces were dear to me. In a village, even one as small as Saint-Maurice, you just can't get along with everyone.

Gilles De Vigan and Auguste Prunille passed by my table on their way out. 'If you prick me, I bleed wine like the Saône,' I picked up from Auguste, my wine grower neighbour. 'But these *vendangeurs* – they don't have what it takes.' The two had been the best of friends ever since Gilles's daughter got together with Auguste's grandson, and I couldn't help but feel I'd had a hand in that.

Yes, I was at home here. My home *was* here. And I wasn't going to let anyone drive me from it.

Thibault returned to the table with two plates of salade Lyonnaise. The perfect starter for a hot day, but I hoped more was coming as I'd grown quite hungry during my people watching.

'Yep, disgustingly happy,' he declared. 'They're moving in together. Guess where.'

My mouth full of salad, I could only shake my head and raise my eyebrows.

'The house across from Sandrine's.'

I swallowed. 'Oh, so it was them—' Wait. No. This morning, Jeanette still thought Théo was sick.

Beau nodded at my realisation. 'Théo called today. They can get it by next week, but right now, it's still empty.'

My fork crashed to my plate. 'You don't think they're keeping an eye on us, do you?' I glanced around the restaurant, afraid I'd suddenly recognise one of Franck's goons.

Beau huffed, mocking my ignorance. 'Of course he's keeping an eye on us. How else would he have known we'd be at Capucine's?'

The salad turned sour in my stomach. I imagined Franck right outside Capucine's villa while we were in there, talking. All my contentedness of a minute ago disappeared.

'In that case, this is my last night at Sandrine's. I don't want to endanger her. What if he feels another innocent bystander would just be a casualty of war?'

'I take it you've come to see things the sidekick's way? Even though they're always wrong?' He gave me a sulky pout that made me laugh and banished some of my apprehension.

'You know I didn't mean it that way. You solved Seive's wife's murder, all by yourself. If only you'd also apprehended him, then perhaps Cyprien wouldn't be dead now.'

'Don't tell me you're mourning the loss of Cyprien.'

'So maybe I won't miss him. But I can't celebrate any death, especially a violent one. Even Cyprien's. You think that's Seive's doing?'

He shrugged. 'It stands to reason that Franck and Seive aren't exactly buddies right now, with Seive making a bid for the throne Franck wants.' He looked up. 'Ooh, does that make me the crown prince?'

'Focus, young sidekick, or I'll turn you into a frog. I think there's a good chance Seive, or more likely one of his friends, arranged that car fire.'

'Which would mean he's still around, handing out orders.'

I nodded. If Seive was against Franck, could that make him our ally? It would be so useful to know whether Patrick Fouquet, the reigning king, knew of all these plots against him, and if he did, whether he'd be inclined to be on our side. The side of his own son. Then again, it was his own brother plotting his demise, according to Beau, so family ties didn't always matter.

'Do you think we could find out where Seive is?' Beau asked.

I frowned. 'Why? Could he be of any use to us? Just because he doesn't like Franck? Besides, if we did find him, he'd have to go to jail. Don't think that would make him inclined to help us. But I don't see how we could ever work out where he is, anyway, if neither the police nor your family have been able to locate him.'

He nodded but seemed oddly disappointed, keeping his gaze down. A waitress came to remove our plates and asked if we wanted anything more, but my appetite was gone, and apparently, so was Beau's.

'I think that for our own peace of mind, we should find out what we can about Delphine. You know, to eliminate the impossible?'

He nodded slowly, then with more determination. 'Sounds like you have a plan.'

'I think we should start by talking to Océane.' With the added bonus that I could gauge whether she wanted to cancel her session or not. I hadn't dared ask Capucine about that, and frankly, I hadn't cared this morning, but I took it as a good sign that my business was starting to matter to me again.

'Hey, you two. Anne-Colombe is taking me back, so if you're ready to go...?' Astrid was glowing with what I suspected was a light alcohol-induced high, her silly big lips spread into a wide smile.

Beau jumped up and went ahead to where Anne-Colombe was waiting. I was less eager to return to the strangers in Sandrine's house but also didn't want to be left behind.

'So, err... you and Beau?'

That was one question I would not miss once he left. But from Astrid, I sensed no judgement, good or bad, so I smiled. 'No, he's taken.'

She giggled. 'Makes sense. He's something, isn't he?'

Her candidness made me laugh. 'Yes, he is definitely something.' Whatever it was.

17

You are my sunshine

There it was again. Just as I had been drifting off to sleep, my room was bathed in light. Whether Sebastian was right in saying the weather was going to turn or not, it was still oppressively hot and my shutters were wide open.

I stared at the ceiling, trying to decide if I should check it out or not. It must be quite late by now. When I'd told Sandrine Beau and I would be leaving in the morning, Emile had suddenly turned into a sociable host, bringing out several expensive bottles of wine to give us what he called 'a tasting journey'. At first, I'd tried to keep up with the 'experience' of fruity high notes and lower, grounded notes of coffee, but in the end, I didn't care if I had a mouthful of tannins or whether the aftertaste was bold. My head was spinning, and I really wanted to talk to Léon.

But when I'd tried to call him, he hadn't picked up. He didn't answer my messages either, which he usually did if a call came at a bad time. He knew I was scared. Why wouldn't he pick up? This had never happened before, and it was the worst time for it. Feeling even lower, I'd tried to fall asleep, but all I could do was toss and turn, on the edge of sleep but not resting.

Photos of Michel Seive I'd seen in the news mixed with the ever-present image of Delphine on my porch. Capucine poured Emile's wine over a burnt-out car that caught alight... No, it was that light again. I sat up, more annoyed than scared at this point. Could I get a break already? I needed my sleep!

I slipped out of bed, avoiding the beam through the window, and peeked around the window frame. Well, there was the light. Coming from the empty house. But not from inside the house. Someone was deliberately shining a light at the villa. At – I checked my smartwatch – two thirty in the morning.

But had Sandrine not said that only Beau and I had bedrooms on this side of the house? I glanced at the wall between Beau's room and mine. He'd been in the car with me. The car with the broken brakes. They... *were* cut, right? My teeth chattered, and I reached for my blouse. I'd been dozing in the car. And I hadn't checked under the bonnet afterwards. Why would I? I had no idea what a brake line looked like. I just about knew the car wasn't powered by tiny horses running on a treadmill. If Beau said the brakes were cut, then they were. He wouldn't just crash my car for fun. Or to scare me. Would he?

I tiptoed to the connecting door between our rooms and opened it slowly so I could peek inside. No Beau. All I could see was an empty bed. I risked opening the door a little further so I could see the window, but Beau wasn't there either. Quickly closing the door, I retreated to my own room and hopped to the other door in a tiptoed run.

Of course, the door opened to the wrong side, so I had to carefully glance around the post to check the rest of the corridor. Beau was at the window in nothing but his shorts. One hand was on the blanket on the chair in front of him, with the other he rubbed his arm. Staring at the light still blinking at the house, he had no idea I was watching him, but my stomach constricted. Why was he there and not at his own window? Was someone messaging him with the light? Was it about me?

I closed the door and leaned against it, panting. How long was I going to pretend everything was fine? I'd seen so many little things about Beau that either seemed just a little bit off or made me feel funny. But every time, I'd been able to tell myself it was just the situation we were in, or it was the age difference, or the difference in background. How much longer could I feign ignorance?

And if I gave in to not trusting Beau any more, where did that leave me? Had I had the enemy under my roof all this time? What had he learned that I shouldn't have shown him?

But if he *was* with them, what could they possibly want from me that required months of surveillance?

I took a few deep breaths. Maybe I was panicking. It was the middle of the night, and I was tired and freaked out by these lights. What if I convinced myself, just one more time, that Beau had also been curious? That there was a good reason for him to be out in the corridor instead of in his room? If he had been the one to open the door, that could have been me, staring at the lights. Would he have panicked if he saw me there? Of course not. But my family came from quite different stock than his.

I bit my lip. Hard. Had I seriously just judged my assistant by his family's social standing? But then, his family was Franck. Well, contained Franck. I paced to the window and back again, biting the nail of my thumb. Thibault was not Franck. I shouldn't make the mistake of seeing them in the same light. But then why was he looking at the light signals?

Maybe I should confront him. I stopped pacing and stared at the door. What could he possibly do, attack me? Ridiculous. But my thumb went back to my mouth. If he did attack me, I'd have no chance. I'd seen those muscles work. They were not for show. He could easily—

Grunting, I pulled my hand away from my mouth. Ridiculous! It was just the dark making me think these stupid thoughts. I stalked to the door and threw it open. Ready to have some serious words with my assistant, I stared at the empty chair in the empty hallway. The light was still signalling.

'You look awful.'

I would have preferred to go downstairs by myself, but Beau was waiting in the chair I'd seen him standing at the night before when I came out of my room. 'Couldn't sleep.' *All because of you*. It might be true, but even if I said it, he would just misinterpret those words. Arrogant little...

'Oh, lovely, are you going to be grumpy all day? Because in that case, I have something better to do.'

'So go do it.'

Of course, he didn't. Instead, he did that thing I hated so much: act extra cheery just to get at me.

'You are my sunshine, my only sunshine,' he sang loudly and off-key.

What I should do was mention Céline. That would teach him. But that was too evil, even for sleep-deprived, grumpy me. Over breakfast, I studied him while he chatted to Astrid and Sandrine. He even managed to draw a few words from Natalya.

Emile came in to kiss his wife goodbye. He and his colleagues were off on some work-related thing, Sandrine explained. Emile produced a bottle of one of the expensive wines he had us drink the night before. 'Here,' he said, 'have this. I like to gift all my guests a little something they'll enjoy. Keep it for a nice occasion.'

I thanked him, and he left.

'Are you sure you'll be okay?' Sandrine asked. 'You can stay as long as you like. It's no trouble.'

I smiled, wondering if I really did look as awful as Beau had said. 'I think it'll just get harder to go home the longer I postpone it. Perhaps being there will trigger a memory that will make everything fall into place and allow us to solve the case.'

Though that would be perfect, I didn't actually believe it. I'd gone over everything that happened at the party so many times now, I would never forget. The real reason I wanted to leave was that I couldn't help but think the light signals were about me. Had they not started when I came? Staying here was no safer than staying at my own house, but at least it was just me there. Well, and Beau.

I looked at him again. In the bright morning light, there was nothing scary about him. He was working that gorgeous smile of his to full effect, and I so wanted to believe he was on my side. But I'd been right the night before. I'd had one too many moments of doubt. I'd be a fool to keep believing in his innocence.

But how guilty was he? Last night, in the dark, the thought had even occurred to me that he could have snuck into my house, grabbed my shoe, and...

But even in that low hour, I'd rejected the possibility. There was absolutely no way Beau was involved with Delphine's death. Nobody was that good an actor. Still, the thought of our accident being fake wouldn't leave me. But if it was fake had it been Beau's idea or had Franck asked him to do it? And why scare me that way? Could it be that Jacqueline was right, that Franck really wanted me to look into Seive's disappearance? But what could *I* possibly find that neither the police nor the Fouquet network could uncover?

Besides, the accident was only the latest thing. Beau had been living with me for months, even before Franck was released. What could be worth going undercover for ten, eleven months? The only one who would have known back then what Seive was planning was possibly Michel Seive himself. And even if Franck *had* known about it, why would he send Beau to live with me? There could be no connection there. I must be missing something...

My brain hurt, and it was only nine in the morning. I asked Sandrine for some paracetamol, then got ready to leave. Beau would take his Harley, so I called my mother to give me a lift. She'd been scared stiff after the accident and had not stopped texting me, so she was happy to be able to do something.

She hugged me tightly when she arrived, asking question after question that I couldn't answer. What happened? Who had cut the brake lines? Why was all this happening to me? There was only one question I *could* answer, but since she was my mother, I lied.

'I'm fine, *Maman*.'

'You're not planning to get any more involved, are you? You've been lucky up till now, but look where it's got you,' she said as she carried Beau's bag to the house.

I followed with my own suitcase, trying to ignore the irritation at her implication that somehow, this situation was my own fault. That was only the case if Franck had actually killed Delphine.

I stopped dead on my doorstep. That was it. I decided then and there that Franck could not have killed Delphine. The whole thing made no sense to begin with. And if I were not at fault, Franck could not be involved. There. I only had to find the real killer now.

Wearing a beatific smile, I joined my mother in the kitchen.

'Happy to be home?'

'Yes, actually. Yes, I am,' I said honestly.

'You're trying to avoid me.'

Crap. I thought I'd succeeded in doing so sneakily. When Beau arrived home – apparently it would take more than suspicion for me to feel that my house *wasn't* his home – I had taken my suitcase upstairs to unpack. I'd only come down once I'd seen him cross the courtyard. I myself had yet to venture out there. I'd gone to my office in my studio through the front doors of both my house and my studio, thereby cleverly avoiding both the area where I'd found Delphine and the view from Beau's window.

But I'd failed to hear him come down in time and was presently only half hidden under my desk.

'I told you, I did not sleep well.' Sighing, I emerged from my hiding place and sat down on my chair.

'Yes, and so I should be avoiding you, not the other way round. What's wrong?'

You. You and your whole family. Even my own thoughts were now making me grumpy. 'Aren't you bothered by the fact that we're being manipulated and we don't even know why?' Unless, of course, he did know and was simply not telling me.

He took his time answering. And when he did, it was with a question. 'Have you been out to the courtyard yet?'

'What's that got to do with anything?'

'Have you?'

'No. But—'

He held out his hand. 'Come on. We'll go together.'

'No. Why?' I sounded like a recalcitrant child, but with his hand out like that, he made me feel like one. Why didn't he just answer my question?

'Come on.' He closed and opened his hand a few times, then held it out again.

He was being infuriatingly patronising in my own office, and I wanted to kick him. But I also wanted to show him I could be just as cool-headed as he was and walk across my own courtyard with my head held high.

So, I got up, shoved him aside, and opened the door to the courtyard before I could think any more of it. Of course, then I was faced with the sight of my porch. The same porch as always. I slowly approached, but my porch remained the same.

'She's not there, is she?'

I didn't answer. Just stared.

'What were you doing?'

His words came floating into my brain as if from very far away. 'Huh?'

'Just now. What were you doing?'

The gravel on the ground came back into focus. There was no body. No more Delphine. Not even on my porch. Someone had taken her away. Her life. That was never theirs to take. My hands started shaking, followed by my arms, my legs, my whole body. I was not afraid. I was raging with anger. How dare they!

Taking someone's shoe was one thing, but taking someone's life!

Though I'd dealt with murder before, somehow it had never hit me like this. I had wanted justice then, but now, it felt more like revenge was the thing I craved. I put my hand to my chest and took a faltering breath. Then another, and another, until I felt mistress of myself once more.

'I was looking at the pictures from the party. To see if there was anything we might have missed.' I was surprised at how calm I sounded, but Beau looked me in the eye, breaking into a slow smile.

'That does not sound like someone who is being manipulated to me. That sounds like something Julie Belmain would do, whether anyone liked it or not.'

I blinked at him. He said it to make me feel better, but he meant it, and he was right. Whatever ulterior motives he had to be here right now, he was not all bad. The fury inside me calmed to a manageable storm. I would find Delphine's killer. And bring them to justice. Because I might be the only one who could.

'Beau, I love you.'

At my words, he visibly stiffened, and I sighed. So much for my heroic resolve. I couldn't even say something dramatic to my sidekick without him taking it the wrong way. So not the reaction I needed right now.

'Chill, I meant as a tenant. Or employee. Or whatever platonic thing you want to be.'

'Anything but a sidekick, really.'

I grinned as I walked away from him.

18

As a witness or as a suspect?

With renewed, anger-filled energy, I sat myself down at my desk. Beau pulled up a chair and joined me.

'So, what are we looking for?' he asked.

I shrugged. 'Anything we don't already know?' I had no idea what we could possibly find in these photos, but if we found anything at all, it would be worth it. We had so few other clues to go on. 'You were in the studio around the time Delphine went missing, but I take it you didn't see anything out of the ordinary either?'

'If I had, I would have told you. But Franck showing up like that rattled me too. It's not always easy being as charming as I am, you know. Just then, it took some effort.'

I smirked and returned to staring at my screen. Seeing all these smiling faces felt a bit unreal. Nobody knew what was happening outside, probably at the very moment the picture was taken. Which meant that anyone actually in the picture could not be the killer. In my mind, I struck people off the list: Marie was talking to Agathe and Maxine. Anne-Colombe was pointing out Yolande to Astrid. The next photo showed Chantelle and Lela admiring one of my pictures on the wall. Nienke had a portrait all by herself, toasting Beau behind the camera with a glass of champagne. A rather awkward photo of Natalya and Sandrine together on the white leather couch at least let them off the hook too.

So who was left? Capucine had been in my office at that moment, but where was Océane? She had been with me in the office as well, but by that time, she should have reappeared in the studio. I clicked ahead to the moment Océane slipped back into view, about five minutes later. By then, Capucine was also literally back in the picture.

'Do you remember seeing Océane around this time?' I asked Beau, but he shook his head.

'It's only five minutes. Even if I had been keeping an eye on the time, there were so many people there. And like I said, I was still wondering what Franck's game was.'

Five minutes... Would it be enough to enter my house, find my shoe, kill a person, and slip back in unnoticed? Even if she didn't know where my shoes were, it wasn't too difficult to find my bedroom, and my shoes were exactly where you'd expect them: at the bottom of my closet. Still, a knife would have been so much more convenient. It would have been easier to find, too, *and* on the ground floor, so with quicker access. No, the shoe must have some kind of significance.

'Do we have a picture of Océane's shoes?' I asked, more for Beau's benefit, as I was the one doing the clicking.

There was a picture that showed Océane's shoes, but they were ordinary sandals. Nice ones, with thin straps, and probably expensive, but nothing exceptional or striking. Maybe Delphine's shoes? I browsed back in time to the moment Delphine was still there. Seeing her face made me pause. Again, I promised I would find her killer, this time to her face. It was different, somehow.

She was in a few other photos before then as well, but none that showed her shoes. In one, she glanced disapprovingly at my art. The next, she had realised the camera was trained on her, and she'd produced a demure smile, pushing her hair back behind her ear with the hand on which she wore the ring with the big, yellow gem. It paired well with the yellow linen dress she wore, but the dress was so long, it obscured her shoes.

Frowning, I hit the forward button again and again. In every picture she was in, there was the dress, there was the ring. A little yellow purse hung off her wrist and showed in a few photos, but no shoes.

I leaned back. 'I give up. I don't know why they used a shoe.'

'You said we should talk to Océane. As a witness, or as a suspect?'

I stared at the photo on the screen. It was the last one taken of Delphine. She was standing in between Capucine and

Océane, and all three were smiling at the camera. What were they really thinking?

'Perhaps Capucine might have ideas about that. They were all in the same club, so she may know whether Océane liked Delphine or if there was any friction between them.'

Putting my words into action, I picked up my phone and called Capucine.

'Julie, so sweet of you to call.' Capucine smiled at the camera. 'How are you?'

'I'm... all right,' I lied. She didn't need to know about all my worries over Franck and Thibault. 'You're looking much better.' In fact, she looked happier than I'd seen her, even at the *vide-grenier* before any of the bad stuff happened.

'Thank you. I feel lighter. I feel like Delphine has forgiven me. You know, for inviting her, and bringing her to her... to your party.'

I wished I could say that. To me, it still felt like *my* party had killed her. But rather than wallow in self-pity, I got to the point. 'I'm happy for you. Also, I have a bit of an odd question. Do you remember what shoes she was wearing on the day?'

Beau raised his eyebrows, so I shrugged one shoulder. All right, it wasn't what I'd said I'd ask, but I still wanted to know.

Capucine blinked, then stared at something off-screen. 'No, I don't think so. She had on a yellow dress, didn't she? I know she had a pair of silver mules. I imagine she wore those, but I can't say I remember.'

'Hm.' I tried not to sound too disappointed. 'Yesterday, your friend Constance said Delphine knew some other people at the party. Do you know who?'

'Oh, yes, of course. Three of your guests belong to our *association*: Océane, Yolande, and Anne-Colombe.'

'So they were friends?' Not according to Constance, but I wanted to hear what Capucine thought.

She pursed her lips. 'I wouldn't say *friends* exactly… I mean, there are quite a few ladies in the club. You can't be friends with all of them.'

'But they were on friendly terms?'

Again, she hesitated, putting her fingers to her lips. 'Mostly, yes. I mean… Well, you remember Constance said she didn't like Delphine?'

As I remembered, Capucine had said Constance didn't like Delphine, but I nodded, my thoughts concentrating on something else now.

'Delphine could be a bit… contrary. She was used to getting what she wanted, and when someone didn't immediately oblige, she could get… strong-willed.'

I waited till she was done talking, only half hearing what she said, as I'd remembered something I now really wanted to ask her about. 'Your ring… In my photos, Delphine is wearing it.'

Capucine paled, her gaze shooting to where I imagined her hand would be. 'Ah. Yes. I lent it to her. Like I said, she was difficult to ignore. But it *is* mine.'

'Of course. It's just something I noticed, that's all. Do you know of any other people who might have disliked Delphine's strong will, as you put it?'

'Oh, I don't like to gossip. Besides, they weren't there, were they?'

Not as far as we knew. But could Océane have let someone in? Five minutes would have been plenty to sneak out and show someone into my house. Although where she would have found a key...

'Let me be blunt, then. What do you know of the relationship between Delphine and Océane?'

Capucine frowned. 'That's very specific. Do you think there was ill will between them?'

'That's what we're trying to find out.'

'But I thought the police were looking at Franck Fouquet.'

'As far as we know, he had no motive. Didn't even know Delphine. We're hoping to establish whether any of the people there who did know her might have had a reason to want your friend dead.'

'I see.' She paused. 'I don't know, actually. I've never seen anything off between them, but to be honest, Delphine and I had never been close before. We were only recently drawn together. I knew her from the club, of course, but we weren't really friends then. She didn't seem to have many. Or any, really.'

'Is that why you became friends?' Beau asked.

'No... Well, in a way. She took an interest in me, and I felt a bit sorry for her, so I suppose you could say...'

'That's why you brought her to the party and not one of your better friends,' Beau concluded.

Capucine winced, and I gave him a withering glance to scold him for being so inconsiderate, then picked up the conversation to cover his faux pas. 'Thank you for giving us that information. It can't have been easy for you, but I'm glad you're feeling better.' If indeed she still was.

But she sat up and gave an airy smile. 'Of course. Anything for justice. *Bonne chance* with your enquiries. Especially on a day like this. Isn't it muggy? And so early too.'

I thanked her again and we said our goodbyes.

Beau leaned back. 'Waste of time. We still don't know any more.'

'Not true. We now know Capucine and Delphine weren't all that close.'

He raised an eyebrow. 'Is that going to help us?'

I shrugged. 'You never know. We've thought things were insignificant before, and they turned out to be vital.'

'You'll see, it'll be some other insignificant thing that's going to turn out vital to this case.'

'Aren't you a ray of sunshine today. Oh, Jacqueline's calling me. Let's see what she wants.'

Beau leaned forward again so he could see my screen as Jacqueline came into view.

'Listen to this. Cyprien Gréban was actually Michel Seive!'

Beau and I exchanged a look.

'No, he wasn't. They were nothing like each other,' Beau said.

'No, no, no. In the car! It was Gréban's car that burnt out, but the person inside was Seive.'

'Oh.' None of us said any more. We all realised the implications of that statement. Seive was no longer missing, but now Cyprien was. Only nobody had any particular reason for wanting Cyprien out of the way, so the logical conclusion was that Cyprien had killed Seive and then fled.

'That's one case solved, then.' It didn't make much of an impact on me. Cyprien had always scared me. That he'd finally crossed the line to murder didn't surprise me, and that he had likely fled far away was only to my advantage.

'And you were right to begin with, Beau,' Jacqueline said. 'The symbolism of the second hand worked out: Seive should have stayed a second.'

Frowning, I bit my lip. 'That's what keeps bothering me. The symbolism. The second hand was a clear message, but what's up with the shoe? If both are meant to mean something, does it follow that both Seive and Delphine were killed by the same person?'

I didn't say it, but we all knew that Cyprien would probably have killed on Franck's order, so we were back to accusing Franck of Delphine's death as well, even if it was by a second hand, as it were.

Beau stood up and left without a word.

'Wha...?' Jacqueline started, but I had no answer. Then I heard his Harley start and drive off.

19

We all need someone

'What's with the shoe?'

Thibault had driven straight to his parents' home, stormed past his mother without greeting, and burst into his sister's room. Ariëlle was lying on her bed, one leg pulled up, scrolling on her phone, the pink and fluffy decor clashing with her dark soul.

Unfazed, she looked up. 'What shoe?'

'Thibault? What's going on?' His mother had followed him, a worried look on her face.

He now turned to her. 'Nothing, *Maman*. I'll tell you later. It's just something between Ariëlle and me.'

Obviously unconvinced, she frowned at him, but years of living with Patrick Fouquet had taught her when to stay out of things. Beau hated seeing the hurt look in her eyes, but he also didn't want to involve her. Gently, he pushed her away and closed the door.

'Oh, she's going to love you for that,' Ariëlle commented. 'She gave up on me years ago, but you were always still salvageable.'

He approached the bed, looming over her. 'You're not as tough as you think.'

She sneered, unimpressed. 'I'm tougher than you think. I'm not like you. I don't care.'

'Says the girl asking me for help for her friend.'

She might not think them similar, but even though she'd been gone for years, he knew her well enough to find the weak spots.

Her gaze turned cold. 'We all need someone.'

'Hm.' He didn't need to point out she'd just contradicted herself. She knew as well as he did that he'd won the first battle. 'So, the shoe to the temple. Why?'

'How should I know? Why are you asking me that?'

'Because I'm sick of this!' He heard his volume rise and took a breath to regain control. 'You know better what's going on than I do, and you weren't even here. I'm sent to look for the key because Julie will trust me, but I'm hardly there before I find out that Cyprien is looking for a house near Saint-Maurice, meaning they didn't trust me from the very start. He's been looking over my shoulder every step of the way, even before Uncle Franck was released. With every key I gave him, he had a new insult for me, until I gave him the antique ones that Julie framed. Then he finally got my point.'

'You could have just said you couldn't find the right key.' Ariëlle's tone was bored, but she sat up to listen, so he joined her on the bed.

'I did. Duh. But he said Uncle Franck wanted me to stay. Never said why. But then he starts threatening her. Leaving her father's ring on the kitchen table? Subtle. Not. I mean, she thought her boring economics teacher had left it for her, so Cyprien's threat backfired and she was actually happy to have it back. But I knew. And it still makes no sense to me. Why scare her? So she'd leave the house? They've been through it a million times, with her there and without. The key is not there. So why not leave her alone?'

Ariëlle folded her arms around her knees. 'Obviously, if the key is gone, she found it and left it somewhere else. And if she didn't put it with the rest of that dumb collection, she must have known what it was. She's not going to give it up just like that, is she? So of course she needs to be convinced that giving up the key would be better for her health.'

Weirdly, it was refreshing to finally be able to talk about everything that had happened in the last year. Though Ariëlle had a matter-of-fact way of speaking about his family's inter-ference in someone's life that rubbed him the wrong way, at least she could answer some of the questions he'd had. From that standpoint, it seemed no more than logical that Julie had to be pressured.

'But she thinks he wants her dead. She doesn't know he's still looking for that key.'

'Doesn't she?'

He stared at her angelic face, framed by a halo of blonde hair. She questioned the one thing he'd seen as a constant through all this: Julie's trust in him. He'd seen Julie waver at times, but he always managed to get her over her doubts. She'd included him in her life completely. He would have noticed if she kept something from him. Wouldn't he?

'She doesn't,' he said more confidently than he felt. 'She's still too afraid, however much she's trying not to be. You should have seen her on the day of Franck's release. She was devastated that I wasn't at her party. But for some reason, it was imperative that *I* would come to pick up Uncle Franck.'

'To show your loyalty.' Ariëlle nodded as if it was the most natural thing in the world. 'You'd been under her influence for months. He needed to know he could still trust you.'

Beau threw up his hand. 'Which he didn't do anyway, because he had me shot.'

'Shot *at*.' She held up a finger. 'I only hit your helmet.'

His mind went blank. He could only stare at her.

'What? I volunteered. You know I'm a good shot. That way, I could be sure you wouldn't get hurt. And I told him it was a dumb idea, that you wouldn't go against him, but he was dead set on it, so I said I'd do it.'

'Did...' He cleared his throat when no sound came out. 'Did you cut the brakes as well?' He knew she was ruthless, but he'd thought she'd have at least some principles when it came to family. Apparently, he was wrong. Or at least, he was wrong about how much their blood relation meant to her. Protecting him by shooting at him was her idea of loyalty.

She laughed. 'Oh, no, that was Franck. He said he'd be in the neighbourhood.'

'But you knew about it.'

She pushed against his shoulder. 'Hey, you're my brother. I look out for you. I make sure he doesn't go too far.'

Beau raised his eyebrows. '*This* is not too far?' She shrugged and he shook his head. 'I'm done. I don't know why he wants to keep me there, but I feel useless. He doesn't trust me to do anything, but in the meantime, his problems are now coming Julie's way, and I can't...'

He trailed off. What was it he wanted? On whose side was he, anyway? He'd thought going to live with Julie would be a good way to get out of all the scheming and plotting. And be closer to Céline. But while he'd loved seeing her every day, he was no closer to her than a year before. What if the pull of Franck's downward spiral expanded to include her? Franck had already shown innocent bystanders meant nothing to him, because in spite of what Julie and Ariëlle said, there was no doubt in Beau's mind that Franck had killed Delphine. And Beau had been right there, unable to prevent it. If only he could—

'Help her?'

Beau turned to his sister, ready to defend himself, pretend he didn't care, but Ariëlle showed some unexpected sympathy.

'Thibault, you're not one of us. You know it. We all know it. You're more like Mum. You want to see the good in people. You don't think their stupidity is our gain. I think that's your stupidity, but hey.'

He laughed in spite of himself and pushed her over.

'Seriously, though,' she said, pushing herself back up, 'you shouldn't be involved in this. Why are you still here?'

'*You* asked me to get Julie to look into Seive's disappearance.' Of course, that only accounted for the last few days, and he knew very well she meant months, if not years.

'I did, but you must have heard they found Seive?'

Beau nodded. 'So did that let your friend off the hook?'

She wrinkled her nose and stared at her toes. 'Not really. I mean, she's his daughter, but they hadn't seen each other in years. And then suddenly his blood is found in her house? It looks dodgy as—'

'But the police are looking for Cyprien.'

She looked up. 'Why? He didn't do it. Well, he may have, but he was tailing me when the car was torched. He thought I didn't know, but seriously, the man is a moron.'

So Franck had been with Julie, and Cyprien also had an alibi. 'But why was he tailing you?'

'Because, dear brother, Franck doesn't trust anyone. I'm friends with Seive's daughter, so my loyalty is questionable, same as yours. Except, unlike you, I don't care. Why do you think I'm here? I'm on the winning side, aren't I? Whatever Franck is doing, it's not going to end well. So here I am, back in Dad's good graces.'

'You don't think all this switching sides is going to leave you without allies?'

She waved a dismissive hand.

'You're reckless.'

'No, confident.' The sneer was back, but Beau got the feeling it was directed at the rest of the world now, rather than at him. He wished he had that kind of confidence. But Ariëlle was right. He didn't belong here. He could never make something of himself here, either with the family or outside of it. Moving to Saint-Maurice hadn't worked. It was too close by, and his family still had their hold over him.

And then there was Céline. She was the one who knew him best. Without giving away the specifics of why he was in Saint-Maurice, he'd opened up about anything and everything he wished and regretted. He'd listened to her own hopes and fears, rejoicing in how close they were to his own, but after every one of those talks he hoped would bring them closer together, she'd acted exactly the same as before. A year of loving her more and more, but he had nothing to show for it but the pieces of his own broken heart.

'I'm leaving,' he said to his sister, who lay down again and picked up her phone.

'Kay, see ya later.'

'Yeah, much.'

She looked at him. 'Oh, I see. *Bon courage*, then.'

He bit his teeth. 'I know you don't care, but as a favour to me, could you keep an eye out for Julie?'

She laughed at first, but when he held her gaze, she rolled her eyes. 'Oh, all right. Softie.'

He left her without more goodbyes, but almost bumped into his uncle when he entered the living room. Franck Fouquet nowadays only entered the house when Patrick was elsewhere, but with Ariëlle returned, he did seem to be here whenever Patrick was not. His moustache as black as his eyes, Franck regarded Beau with his usual disdain.

'Thibault. Good to see you.'

Beau almost slipped back into a generic greeting, but he was beyond caring what his family thought and wanted of him. How this man treated people, and especially a wonderful woman like Julie, filled him with disgust. 'I would return the sentiment, but it hasn't been for years.' He turned away, but his uncle stopped him with a hand on his arm.

'What's got into you?'

'I could ask you the same thing. But I've been talking to Capucine Jamin, and maybe I shouldn't be surprised.'

Franck narrowed his eyes, then loosened his grip and slowly moved back. 'Who?'

Whether or not he recognised the name, Beau wasn't sure, but his own stake in the matter had dropped away. Franck would be judged for what he'd done to Delphine. Julie would see to that. But neither she, nor Franck, nor anyone in this country, needed Beau for anything.

'Just go.' Beau turned his back on Franck, hopefully for the last time, and sat next to his mother on the couch as his uncle left the room. She still wore the worried frown he'd put there earlier.

Not knowing how to say what he had to say without hurting her, he got straight to the point. '*Maman*, I'm going away. You know I met Ken Doo, right, and he has offered me an opportunity. I'm taking it, so I'm going to America.'

To his surprise, his mum's face cleared right up. 'Good!'

'You... *want* me to go?' He'd hurried his words so as not to prolong her worry, but he'd expected her to oppose his plans.

She reached out and covered his hand with hers. 'No, of course not, not like that. I'll miss you very much, but you need to get away. Go somewhere where all expectations are your own. And sooner rather than later.'

He looked her in the eye, not ready to accept her smile. He wanted to tell her how he never felt like he was a full member of the family, but that would only hurt her feelings when it was never her fault he felt that way. He wanted to tell her he was done pretending. Pretending to Julie he'd left the family and was now on her side. Pretending to his family Julie meant nothing to him. Now pretending he wasn't scared or upset about his family's guilt in a murder so Julie would do her sleuthing for someone she didn't even know existed…

If he was going to pretend, he might as well get paid for it. Appreciated for it instead of despised. He wanted to tell his mum all that, but he couldn't find the words. And then… she already knew. He suddenly realised just how similar they were.

'Come visit me?'

She laughed. 'Don't tempt me. I might stay.'

'I'll get a big apartment.' He finally managed a grin, and she folded him into the warm hug he so desperately needed.

20

Had I missed anything?

To go, or not to go? Without wanting to get overly dramatic, I'd had that question on my mind for the past fifteen minutes. The man from the garage had dropped off a loaner, as they wouldn't get to fixing my beautiful car before the end of August, when all the employees would return. Now, in possession of transportation, I'd messaged Océane and she'd agreed to meet me in town, but I hadn't heard from Beau since he'd stormed off. I would have to go within the next few minutes if I was going to make it in time, but I didn't know if I should wait for Beau or not.

Time crept by, and I sent Beau another text, but in the end, I had to leave without him. Océane had picked a delightful tearoom on the river to meet, though for my tastes, it was a little on the exclusive side. The ladies meeting in this establishment were all more mature than me, more expensively coiffed than me, and decidedly more beige than me. My red-on-white polka dots stood out from the moment I entered. Some ladies appre-

ciated my splash of colour and smiled. Others conspicuous-
ly did not.

Still, this place was at least open, and cool inside. Many
of the restaurants and cafés closed in August, when all of
France went on holiday. With the unending heatwave that
today had turned humid and sticky under a cloudy sky,
moods were too low for people to go out and meet each
other, so it was a miracle Océane had found somewhere that
served cake.

Océane, in turquoise with dark blue accents, had opt-
ed for something in between my loudness and the other
patrons' plainness when it came to dress, making her the
queen of the tearoom in my eyes. She waved me over to the
table near the window where she sat.

'Lovely to see you. I take it this isn't about my upcoming
photo shoot?'

I lowered myself on the seat opposite her, taking those
few seconds to fast-forward to the point as well. 'Not one
for small talk, are you?'

Her lips formed a smile, but her eyes, though intelligent
and indulgent, did not join in. 'After all that happened, I
think we're beyond that, don't you? It would only get harder to talk about the unpleasant thing you want to mention
if we started off with a light-hearted conversation about the
bavarois, delicious as it may be.'

Her words were timely, as the waitress came to take our orders. After that, I had to try the *bavarois*, a smart sweet treat to serve on a day like this, as it was chilled and not baked.

'I'd like to ask you how well you knew Delphine,' I said after the waitress had left. It wasn't the most burning question, but as much as she wanted to come to the point, I couldn't come out and accuse her simply because she wasn't in any of my pictures from the party.

'I tried to get her removed from the Ladies' Association. That's how well I knew her.'

My eyebrows shot up, and I blinked a few times. For all her sophisticated behaviour, Océane sure didn't mince words.

'She tried to blackmail me. And since nobody in the club liked her, I assume she tried it before and after me as well.'

'Tried?' It seemed impolite to push, but I had to know if I was going to get anywhere in this investigation.

'She found out about an indiscretion in my youth, but that had been long settled with everyone involved. It could still hurt my reputation, but I called her bluff. I'm sure not everyone had the courage to do so. I almost didn't, myself.'

'Do you know of anyone else she approached?'

She paused, sizing me up. 'I do, but I won't give you their names, if you don't mind.'

'Of course. But did you contact any of them to say Delphine was at my party?'

She frowned. 'What would be the point of that?'

The waitress brought our coffee and *gateau*, so I had a few moments to consider her answer. Though it was a counter question and not a direct denial, it had come so quickly that I believed her response was genuine. In which case, if she did have anything to do with Delphine's death, the implication was that she'd done it herself.

'You're right, the *bavarois* is excellent.' Its velvety coolness alone dispelled any thoughts of the clingy heat outside, but a hint of hibiscus cut through the sweet fruit to elevate the flavour from good to give-me-a-minute.

'You think Delphine was attacked by someone she blackmailed.' Océane hadn't touched her *gateau*. Perhaps there was something of the sociopath in her, after all.

'Did the police not ask you any of this?' Just because they hadn't been in touch with me didn't mean they weren't questioning other people. Though it seemed strange they never got back to me on the brake lines after I'd reported the accident. I specifically mentioned the murder investigation, but the officer had seemed rather unimpressed.

'The police? No. They only wanted to know if I knew... Forgive me, I forget your ex-husband's name. But when I said no, they moved on to the next person. I thought the whole thing must be something to do with him until you sent that message asking to meet.'

So Chagrin also believed Franck killed Delphine. That in itself almost convinced me he hadn't, but at least *I* was already looking into other angles.

'How did you feel when you unexpectedly saw Delphine at my studio?'

An amused little smile appeared on Océane's face. One that did reach her eyes. 'If you're asking whether I got a murderous glint in my eye, I did not. I was there to have fun with my friends. If I had let her ruin that, I'd be the biggest loser.'

While that was wise, I was still left with my most pressing question. 'Then where did you go after you left my office?'

Genuine surprise widened her eyes. 'What do you mean? I went back to the party.'

'You're not in any of the photos right around the time the crime must have been committed.'

All sophistication left her manners as her voice rose to a level that attracted curiosity from the entire tearoom. 'Are you accusing me of...?!' But just as quickly, she regained control. 'Oh, no, wait. I went into the dressing room to look at your collection of petticoats. That blonde woman on drugs saw me, but if you want a more reliable witness, I think Yolande also knew I was in there.' She lifted her chin and gave me a haughty, cold stare worthy of a dethroned princess. 'You'll have to find another suspect.'

She got up and left me with the bill for our half-eaten *gateau*. Taking another bite, I sighed. One fewer client for me. I hoped she wouldn't scare away the rest of the Ladies' Association. More importantly, though, if she was telling the truth, I was yet again without suspects. Apart from the obvious one.

Once my *bavarois* was finished, I paid quietly, ignoring the inquisitive look the waitress gave me about the untouched *gateau*, and drove home over empty roads, pulling my fitted dress away from my body as far as it would go. The oppressive heat was dulling my brain. Had I missed anything? Would Beau have asked questions I hadn't even thought of? Or had considered impolite to ask? It would have made for a neat solution if somehow we could pin this on Océane, but I had to agree with Capucine's friend Constance. Océane was not our killer.

There was only one more question I needed to ask before I would be forced to admit defeat.

I jumped out of my car when I arrived home and hurried into the kitchen. Beau was sitting at the table, hunched over his phone. He looked up and opened his mouth, but I held up my finger.

'In a sec. I just need to— Hi, Capucine.' Pulling out a chair next to him, I made sure Beau could see the screen. 'Just one more question. Was Delphine blackmailing you?'

If I was burning bridges already, I might as well continue. Beau sat up straighter at my question, but Capucine changed colour.

'What? Who said that?'

'I'm afraid I can't—'

'It was Océane, wasn't it? That woman is such a pin. She can hold people together, but she has to stab them in order to do so. Don't listen to her. Jealousy doesn't look good on anyone.'

With that, she hung up.

I widened my eyes at Beau. 'Isn't that interesting?' I asked.

He didn't react as excitedly as I'd hoped. Where had he been in the meantime? Everything about him slumped, from his shoulders to the corners of his mouth. Even his hair seemed limper than usual.

His words came slowly. 'Hm. It all comes down to you, doesn't it? Capucine might have been a suspect, except she was with you when it happened. *You're* now the alibi for the most likely suspect in two separate murder cases. Don't you think that's suspicious in itself?' His words made sense, but his thoughts were elsewhere. The way he was fidgeting with his phone, turning it over and over on the table, he was gearing up to get something off his chest.

'All right, let's have it. Are you leaving?' I might as well rip off my own plaster. I asked the question before I could think about it and start to panic. I'd known he'd be going, but did he have to go *now*?

A faint smile crept over his lips. Though he kept his eyes on the table, he stopped turning over his phone.

'Yes.'

'Now?'

He got up, raking a hand through his hair, paced to the kitchen counter and back to the table, where he sat down on a chair opposite me. I followed him with my eyes, my breath becoming shallower with each movement. Whatever was coming, was it really so bad that he couldn't be near me to tell me?

'I have to. You see…' He took a deep breath and looked me in the eye. 'I lied. I didn't escape my family. I'm only escaping now… hopefully… but I came here on Franck's orders.'

My heart skipped a beat. I'd suspected it, rejected it, and secretly believed it, but hearing it confirmed was still a shock. I sucked in my lower lip to keep it from wobbling while Beau explained.

'To keep an eye on you. And to look for… something.' He looked away again on that last word. 'A key. I shouldn't be telling you this. But I don't see how it could be any less dangerous for you not to know.'

He paused, and I almost physically felt the distance between us grow. If he had come here to spy for Franck, how much did that leave of our friendship? Had it all been an act?

'Ariëlle, my sister, said—'

My jaw dropped. 'You have a sister?'

'We're not close.' He frowned. 'You must have seen her picture, in my parents' house? It's on the wall near the...' He shook his head. 'Anyway. She's been working for Franck, and she doesn't believe he killed Delphine. But that's beside the point.'

He sat up straighter. 'I thought that if I came here, I could keep an eye on you. Not for him, but for you. The way he's been talking about you... He's changed, Julie. He was never great, but now... He seems suspicious of everything. Doesn't even use a smartphone any more. And you're at the centre of his darkness. I didn't know if there would be anything I could do to protect you, but I had to try. For old time's sake.'

I swallowed to get rid of the knot in my throat, but it was a stubborn one. Beau said he'd come for me. But he'd been lying from the very minute he came here.

'The first few months were easy. Nothing much happened. You know about Cyprien trying to worm in on my task, of course. He wouldn't have shown interest in buying a house here in Saint-Maurice without Franck at least knowing of it, so I knew Franck didn't trust me, but he also didn't intervene. So I enjoyed my time away from everyone. I did.' He looked me in the eye to make sure I believed him. 'More than I expected to.'

By now, I was biting my lip. Almost a year he'd been here. For almost a year, he'd lied to me. But hey, at least he'd had fun doing it. I balled my fists, determined to hear him out before I let loose.

'But then, he was released. My father wanted me to be there, which meant I had to miss your party. That's when I realised whose side I was actually on. But I couldn't tell them that. As long as they still thought I was only here to do their bidding, at least I had some idea of what they were planning. I could warn you if things got too hot.'

'So this is you warning me?' I said through gritted teeth, the bitterness obvious even to me.

His jaw muscles worked, but his gaze was fixed on the table in front of him once more. 'Look, you've only seen him twice recently. You think I'm a good actor? That runs in the family. Don't believe a word he says. Prison has not changed him for the better. There's a reason I keep telling you he's a killer.'

He leaned forward on his elbows, folding his hands together. 'The thing is, if it was just you he was frustrated and vengeful about, I think that might have died down eventually, once he got back into daily life. But he has creditors on his tail. They don't care he's been in prison. They want their money.'

Franck needed money? That was a first. As long as I'd known him, he'd always been very careful with money, stingy even. 'I thought he had plenty.'

Beau laughed without humour. 'He does. But it's locked away. He converted it all to cash before they arrested him, so it couldn't be found and confiscated. Put it in a safe deposit box in Villefranche and hid the key.'

Finally, the pieces started to fall into place. 'In my house.'

'Well, in your great-aunt's house, as it was then. It wasn't an obvious place where anyone would think to look, but he figured it would stay in the family. Only my immediate family knows about this. And Cyprien, of course. He didn't have others search the house until it was already yours, so they thought it was something to do with getting revenge on you.'

'But if he hid it, he must know where he put it. Why didn't he just tell you where it was? Why send you to live with me?'

'Obviously, the first thing I did when I came here was check for the key. It was supposed to be under a loose part of the window sill in what is now your guest bedroom, but there was nothing there. And by that time, you'd built up a whole collection of keys. We all thought that you must have found it, realised what it was, and hid it in plain sight. But no matter how often I went through that basket, whenever I found something that might be it, Franck just called me an idiot.

'Now, I know you never found that key. We still don't know what happened to it, but Franck believes you have it hidden somewhere. With everything he did to you, he never underestimated your resourcefulness.' His knuckles turned white.

'I'm afraid that's why you're still alive. As we've seen in the car, he doesn't care whether I live or die, but he thinks he needs you to get to his money.'

'Wait, the accident was real?' My heart beat faster just realising I'd actually escaped death. With the thought that Beau had staged the whole thing, I'd got over it pretty quickly, but the danger of the situation came swooping back to me now.

Beau frowned at me. 'What, you think I'd lie to you about that?'

I only raised an eyebrow.

'Oh. Fair enough. But yes, that was real. As was the bullet in my helmet. Courtesy of my loving sister. Just making sure I remembered where my loyalties were supposed to lie. I guess I'd been too obvious about not wanting to be there when we picked Franck up from prison.'

My eyes widened. What a family. Though my heart rate was still up because of Beau's lies, I had to admit that he hadn't had a great frame of reference on how to act like a decent human being. A father who only ever seemed disappointed in him, an uncle who used him but didn't trust him, and a sister who shot at him to keep him safe. Now I was almost glad he wouldn't be around them much longer. Bit by bit, my fists relaxed. 'So let me get this straight. You didn't do what you were supposed to, because you didn't get the key and you defected. Franck hasn't thought to look for the key elsewhere, as he thinks I'm pulling the wool over his eyes. What I don't get is why he hasn't tried to get his hands on my money, if he's in such desperate need of it.'

'He has.' He said it softly and openly but didn't add any details.

I frowned, remembering everything that had happened in the past months to see if something stood out that could have been Franck's doing, but nothing came to mind. A little flame of pride flickered. I must have learned my lesson well, doing enough to protect my money that even Franck couldn't get to it. But I also realised what the consequences would have been. 'So now he's angry at both of us. And you think he wants to kill me, but you're not going to be around to see it. Is that it? No.' I held up my hand when he wanted to protest. 'I don't mean that as an accusation. If Franck truly wants to kill me, you standing in the way isn't going to make a blind bit of difference.'

Beau hung his head.

I sighed. 'I wish you'd told me sooner, though.'

'If I had, you would have acted differently. You would have searched for the key yourself, or informed Jacqueline, or marched into the bank with your whole basketful of keys. Uncle Franck would have realised you were no longer of use to him and moved on to the revenge part of his plan. I think he's been getting to that conclusion for a while, but with Seive not doing as he was told, Franck had other things on his mind.'

'So Seive was working for Franck. Is that why you wanted me to find him? To have some proof against Franck?'

'With the Bouviers putting pressure on Uncle Franck to deliver their money, and the key firmly lost to him, he had to find some other way of repaying them. He asked Dad, but that was after he'd made the mistake of having me shot at. Even though it was only a "reminder" or "scare tactic" as my sister calls it, Dad wasn't happy that his family was turning on each other. If he can't even control his own family, how is he going to run an organisation, and all that. So no money for Franck. All he did was offer him his old job at the factory, but I think that was more so Dad could keep an eye on him.

'The only other option for Franck was to take over completely. Seive was supposed to be a front, but he saw an opportunity for himself. In a way, that worked out in Franck's favour, because by eliminating Seive, he could return to Dad with evidence of his loyalty. As long as Dad never finds out Seive was supposed to hand the reins to Franck. I thought about telling him, but without proof, I wouldn't get anywhere.

'This, of course, is all information I got from Ariëlle. She was never much of a family person. Her loyalty is to her friends. And one of her friends happens to be Seive's daughter. Ariëlle came to me to ask you to look into his disappearance, and I thought she in turn might be in a better position to protect you. Though with her, there are never any guarantees. I'm only telling you now because I'll have no other opportunity to do so. After Delphine's murder, I think Franck has tasted blood. My sister may not believe he did it, but you are in danger, and I can't help you.'

He stood and moved to the door. Then he hesitated. 'After what I said to him this morning, right now, he's probably angrier with me than with you. So I'm leaving.' He looked me in the eye one last time. 'Goodbye. Thank you... I'm sorry.'

When I heard his Harley start five minutes later, I realised I was still sitting in the same spot, my cheeks wet and my hands shaking.

21

The worst was yet to come

Thibault Fouquet had never felt so miserable in his life. But the worst was yet to come. After today, would he ever see Céline again? Banishing that thought until he had time to die, he parked his Harley and entered the bakery.

'She's upstairs, trying on a new dress,' Monsieur Plaisant said, in between counting out change for a customer. 'Knock!' he shouted after Beau when he was halfway up the stairs. On any other day, the lack of trust would have irked Beau, but with every step he took, only his apprehension grew.

What if she didn't care he'd be gone? Or worse, what if she was happy for him? Should he pretend everything was fine and leave her happy? Apart from keeping things from her, he'd never actually lied to her before. And as he was already leaving, never to see her again, wasn't this his one opportunity to tell her how he felt?

He knocked.

'One second!'

She sounded so pleased. She must really like that new dr—

'Oh! Thibault!' Céline had swung open the door, her light brown hair tumbling over her shoulders. But Beau could only stare at the skin-tight, bright red number that left nothing to the imagination. Céline turned almost as red as her dress, folding her arms then unfolding them, and finally stepping aside to let him in.

He almost forgot he could walk. He'd already forgotten how to talk. Céline's bedroom had never been big, but it was getting smaller by the minute. Was there any distance left between them?

Céline bit her lip in a shy smile. 'What do you think?'

Thinking? What was that, again? He'd come here for a reason, but he couldn't quite remember what it was. 'It's... different.'

Her smile froze.

'I mean, it's not your usual.' She was the girl in pastels and broderie anglaise. Not this centrefold model. Not knowing where to look, he stared out the window.

'You don't like it,' she said softly.

Keeping his eyes on the building across the street, he laughed. 'It's impossible not to like that. It just... takes some getting used to.'

She was silent long enough for him to remember what he'd come to tell her. He wouldn't have time to get used to this new Céline. Someone else would have to appreciate her. He winced. Nobody but him would ever know her well enough to fully appreciate the dream that was Céline.

'Beau...'

He frowned, slowly turning towards her. She'd never called him Beau before. She'd thought it mean when people still said it as a joke and so she'd always used his full name. Now, she stood there, hugging herself, her gaze downcast, changing the habit of a lifetime.

'Why have you never tried to kiss me?'

Her question knocked him off balance. It robbed him of the ability to breathe, let alone answer.

'What's wrong with me, that everybody and their grandmother gets to... And I... I'm always there, but...'

'Nothing! There's absolutely nothing wrong with you.' He finally found his voice and used it before she could heap more doubt on herself. She looked so miserable that he wanted to take her in his arms and show her how perfect he thought she was. But how did this sudden insecurity fit with what she'd said years before? 'You wanted to be just friends.'

He took a step towards her, and she looked up, her eyes moist. 'When did I say that?'

'Five years ago. I said I loved you, and you laughed.' It had taken his heart a while to get over that, but here he was, about to make the same mistake again.

She stared at him, first in disbelief, then slowly remembering. 'We were seventeen! You asked me to marry you! In front of my friend, by the way, who already thought I was crazy for hanging out with you. What was I supposed to do? I thought I could explain later, but then I didn't see you again for two years.'

At least her indignation had banished the self-doubt. With squared shoulders, she now faced him, still in that extremely distracting dress. He'd forgotten about the friend. *Nobody gets married at seventeen*, she'd mocked him. *We have plans, you know.* Giggling, they'd walked away from him.

'I didn't mean marry me there and then.'

'And how was I supposed to know that?'

'Because we were seventeen!' He bridged what little distance there was between them and gathered all his courage. 'I still love you. I still want to marry you. And I still don't mean here and now.'

She glared at him for two more endless seconds in which he wasn't sure if she was going to rant at him or simply send him away. Then she broke into the widest, most glorious smile. 'Shame. I think we're old enough now.'

When his lips finally touched hers, he wanted the moment to last forever. He held her close, trying to rein in his desire to show her with this one kiss how much he loved her and wanted to be with her. But then reality came crashing down on him, and he pulled away.

Panting, she smiled up at him. 'Yay, my dress worked.' But seeing his expression, she shrunk away. 'What's wrong?'

'I... I came to say goodbye. I'm leaving. For America.'

She gave a small shrug, shaking her head. 'Yes? And?' Then realisation hit. 'Oh. You don't want me to come?'

'What? No! I mean yes. I do want you to come. But what about your dad? Your work?'

She placed a hand on his chest. 'Oh, Dad has always known I wasn't going to stay here forever. Baking is nice and all, but I studied social work, remember? I want to do more for people than I can do here. Dad knows that. So maybe he didn't expect me to leave just yet, but he'll get over it. Right now, I just want to be with you.'

The lead weight that had been piling on top of his heart melted away with the fire Céline lit in it. She was coming with him! He repeated it to himself, too stunned at this turn of events to allow himself to believe it. He cupped her face and kissed her again, longer and deeper this time. Still a little afraid she'd come to her senses, he would take all he could from this moment.

But she didn't change her mind. She answered his kiss with a passion that rivalled his own, running her fingers through his hair and pressing her body against him. But when his hand slid down over her back, she flinched.

As if stung, he let go of her, though her own arms were still around him. 'What is it? Something wrong?'

She gave him a cheeky grin. 'Can you unzip me? I think there's a pin left in this dress.'

He laughed and pulled her back into his arms. But halfway down her back, his hand froze on the zip.

That woman is such a pin. She can hold people together, but she has to stab them to do it.

Slowly, he loosened his hold on Céline, who frowned.

'Now what? I thought—'

He gave her a quick kiss, then held up his finger. 'Hold that thought. I... I have to go, but...' Another kiss. 'I *will* be back. Soon.' Kiss. 'Very soon.' He'd already stepped away but turned back for a longer kiss. 'Keep the dress. But don't ever show it to anyone else.' Opening the door, he repeated, 'I'll be back before you know it.'

He was halfway down the stairs when she called after him. 'Thibault Fouquet, come back here right now!'

Everything in him wished he could. Now that he finally had what he'd wanted for so long, he didn't want to give it up even for a moment, but he had to. He couldn't leave Julie at the mercy of a killer.

22

He's a coward!

I was going through the motions of reheating leftovers for lunch, just to have something to occupy myself with. Thibault had made this dish. I wasn't hungry to begin with, but realising that, I wanted to dump it, pot and all, in the bin.

Not knowing whether to feel betrayed, hurt, angry, or abandoned, my soul had settled for empty. I had no feelings left. After Beau left, I'd dried my cheeks, poured myself a glass of water, and called Léon. It was ridiculously early on his side of the ocean, but I needed his comfort more than ever. Only, like the night before, there had been no answer. That had truly made me cry.

I'd spent minutes bent over the kitchen table, sobbing onto my arms, feeling thoroughly lonely, but then the bitterness had set in. Men. I should have known. My ex-husband had come back into my life, and all the men I depended on immediately left me.

A group call with my mother and best friend Tiana had lasted about ten seconds. They were both on their way, which was why I was now trying to be a good hostess and offer them food. But I had been glaring at the pot as if it were the source of all my troubles, instead of heating it.

How could I let this happen? I knew men were useless. Starting with my father, who died on me. And look at my brother. Sure, he was a children's surgeon, which was great. But how long had it taken him to realise he and Maëline should be together, not just living in one house? And how about my neighbour, who murdered his wife and got away with it? Men!

And still, I'd let one into my life, into my house. And of course he turned out to be a lying snake. Had I not known it all along? I only had myself to blame for being stuck with a criminal – possibly murderous – ex-husband, and no one here to help. Beau had said he'd wanted to help. Ha! Where was he now? Fled. Left me to deal with it. By myself.

I sniffled. I needed more pity. Jacqueline was the obvious person, but again, no answer. Was I even a friend to her? What was it with all these people not realising I needed them? What could be more important in their lives?

My front door banged open and knocked over my self-pity. The two seconds it took for my mother and Tiana to envelop me in their warmest hugs were enough for me to realise how extremely selfish I was. How easy it was for me to blame others when I felt bad. And how incredibly grateful I should be to even still have people around me who did care, in spite of those awful traits.

'Have you eaten?' To my mother, food was always the answer. Strangely, she was often right. She let go of me and switched on the heat underneath the pot.

It was as if she'd lit a fire underneath my brain. All the meals from the past days pinged up, together with what people had been telling me. Océane over coffee and cake, Capucine over water and chocolates, Thibault over salads at the hotel.

It was him all along.

But Beau had left. What was I going to do? Panic clawed at my bruised self-worth. Why did he have to go?

Tiana loosened her grip on me. 'Why now?'

'Exactly!' I wailed.

'No, I'm asking. Why did he leave now? If Franck is planning to hurt you, Beau wouldn't leave you when the danger is at its greatest.'

'Oh, wouldn't he?' I almost shrieked. 'He's been here all this time because Franck sent him. He said he wanted to help, but now that Franck's getting closer, he oh-so-conveniently can't do anything more for me. He's a coward!'

My phone beeped. Thinking it might be Jacqueline, I picked it up and gasped. 'He's gone to confront Franck at the factory.'

My mind whirred as my mother and Tiana exchanged glances. What was he planning? When he'd left my house, he'd been utterly defeated but with hopes for a better future elsewhere. What had happened between then and now that had changed his plans?

Céline. She must have turned him down, and he no longer had anything to live for.

In spite of the situation, I huffed a laugh. No, that was ridiculous. I was being dramatic. Something must have convinced him of the same conclusion I had just drawn.

'I have to go help him.' Whatever his reasons were, he had notified me of his actions for a reason.

'No, you don't!' Tiana said, her eyes wide.

'*Maman*, call the police. Ti, you call Jacqueline. I'm going.'

Grabbing my sleeve, Tiana tried to stop me. 'What are you, too stupid to live? You said yourself that Franck is trying to kill you.'

'That was when we'd just had the accident. Beau explained that Franck was only using scare tactics. I mean, if I die under suspicious circumstances, who do you think they'll suspect first? Franck is a lot of things, but he's not stupid.'

I extracted myself from her grip and hurried to my car before they could try something else, like reasoning. Right now, I was too busy to keep my own reasoning at bay to listen to theirs. Was coming to Beau's rescue a good idea? No. Had I not been furious with him less than ten minutes ago? Yes. But the little bit of reason I had left was telling me the police would be there before I got to the factory, so I really didn't need to worry. I'd be there for mental support after whatever was going to happen happened.

Driving down the winding road into the valley, I let everything that had happened over the past couple of days replay in my mind. We still had two murders and a disappearance, though the identity of the disappeared had switched with that of one of the murders. Which probably meant the one was the murderer of the other. But Beau had shone a light on something that had been bothering me too. Why did I seem to be in the middle of all this?

The disappearance and consequent death of Michel Seive would have nothing to do with me, ordinarily. Cyprien had disappeared, and therefore was most likely to be the murderer. But his car, containing the body, had been set alight by someone who looked like Franck, only it couldn't be Franck because he'd been under my watchful eye at the time. That in itself was odd, but he had also been present around the time of a murder in *my* house that should have nothing to do with *him*.

It was too obvious that he was involved in this. And too obvious that he wanted me involved as well. With all this obviousness, I'd begun to doubt. A perfect stranger to me had been killed in my house. Franck had been there, but she'd been a stranger to him too. Scare tactics aside, Franck hadn't threatened me at all. In fact, he'd asked for my help. He was so involved that my residual fear of him had clouded my mind. Beau had been right all along. Franck had killed Delphine, and I was too self-involved to see it.

This murder had been the one I knew most about. We were all there at the party. Capucine and Delphine weren't supposed to be there in the first place, but they did know three people who were invited, only those people had been surprised to see them. So Capucine had not told them she'd be going. And why would she? She didn't know the other club members would be there either. Which all meant this had to be a crime of opportunity.

The motive seemed clear enough: Delphine had been a blackmailer. Océane said Delphine had no hold on her, but she did admit she could still be hurt by what Delphine knew. Capucine had not admitted to being blackmailed, but it was clear that she had been pressured, as demonstrated by the lending of the ring with the yellow stone.

And that little gem had got me thinking. The ring was the evidence I thought was missing from all this. Delphine had been wearing it because it matched her outfit. There was no reason she would give it back halfway through the party, but still Capucine had had it afterwards. The police wouldn't have given it to her during an open investigation, which left only one option: the killer had taken the ring and given it back to Capucine.

An accomplice. But who? Océane? Both women seemed to have reason to want Delphine gone from their lives. But neither would have known where to find my shoe, or have a key to my house.

Which is where Beau's conviction must have come in. He'd said Franck's men had gone over my place time and again to find some key. I'd had no idea, so they must have had a copy of my house key. The studio with all my expensive equipment was locked with three different keys, but with Franck safely in prison, I'd got used to only using one of the locks on my home's front door. I'd made it easy on them!

And knowing Franck, he wouldn't have trusted his men to do the job right. Once he was out of prison, he would have gone straight to my house to look for the key himself. He would have remembered where everything was. It all fit.

The one thing that had thrown me off Franck's trail was that there was no connection between Franck and Delphine. But there was. Capucine had said that she hated Franck, but she'd also said Delphine was her friend. If the latter wasn't true, then perhaps the first had been a lie, and in that case...

I growled in frustration and dug my nails into the steering wheel. Even if those pieces fit together, there was still the issue of why they would involve *me*. I had only met Capucine the morning of the party. They couldn't possibly have known they would even be at my house. Had the whole thing just been a coincidence after all?

But Beau didn't think so. He was convinced Franck was the killer, which meant he was now risking his life in order to prove it. My reasoning said he was right. But was I convinced too? Franck had never killed before, as far as I knew. Beau could be wrong about the whole thing. Which meant there was a chance he was not even in danger.

This was what I kept telling myself as I pulled into the factory parking lot at the north side of Villefranche and parked next to the single police car there. Only two other cars populated the lot. The August holiday season had struck here too. Beau's Harley was next to the entrance, which meant one of the cars was likely Franck's. The other must belong to a guard or a cleaner.

While the sky above me turned darker, memories surfaced from the time Franck and I were still together. He'd had to stop by work sometimes when we were on a date, but I was never allowed in. Over the years, I'd spent hours in this parking lot, and the building still seemed ominous and imposing to me. But this time, I was going in.

My heart pounding, I was vaguely aware that one police car seemed on the meagre side, but I had probably seen too many action movies. Franck was one man, in a relatively public space, dealing with his nephew. The most the police officer would have to deal with was a shouting match. Right?

As I approached the entrance, the first fat drops of rain were starting to fall.

'*Bonjour*. I'm here to see Franck Fouquet,' I said to the receptionist, who had her face turned towards a small desk fan.

With a bored smile, she asked, 'Is he expecting you?'

I gave her a saucy look. 'Let's just say I want to surprise him.'

It could be my imagination, but I thought I saw her nose wrinkle. The woman had taste.

'Now might not be the best time...' she began.

'Oh, you mean the police officer?' I said as airily as I could. Then I leaned over the counter and winked, holding up my hand beside my mouth as I whispered, 'He's not real.'

She studied my face, but I must have picked up some of Beau's skills in the past months, as she pointed up the broad steps to her left. 'Second office on the right.'

I mounted the stairs and sincerely hoped I was correct in assuming the police officer had the situation under control by now. I still hadn't been able to figure out what could have possessed Beau to come barging in here after he'd supposedly broken all ties with his uncle. He must have been seriously convinced of Franck's guilt to go back now. Had he found a new clue? Or was there something I'd missed all this time?

The office with Franck's name on the door had a narrow window beside the door. The light was off, and the room seemed empty, but when I tried the door, it opened, so I went inside, making sure to close the door behind me. If there was any evidence in here, I didn't want Franck to find me before I had found it. Then again, the office was as good as empty, save for a desk with a laptop, a file cabinet with some plastic bottles on top of it, and a sorry-looking plant in the corner.

But then a flash of lightning lit up the office, and I saw the feet.

23

I told Julie

As soon as I rounded the desk, I recognised him. Major Étienne Chagrin. He was lying face down on the carpet, but I saw no injury. I knelt beside him and shook his shoulder – no response. Wincing, I turned him over so I could feel his pulse and breathed a sigh of relief.

So he was alive. But still unconscious. He wasn't going to be any good to me. Thunder rolled outside as I took out my phone and hesitated. Emergency services, or straight to the police station? The alarm call would only go to the station, right? Might as well cut out the middleman.

The officer answering the phone sounded bored. Well, he was about to wake up. 'I'm at the Purinett factory and I've found Major Chagrin.'

'Ah, good.' He sounded bored as ever, and was he eating something? It might be lunchtime, but he was at the front desk.

'No, not good. He's been knocked out. You need to send backup.'

'Calm down, madame. Someone is already on their way to the factory. Don't worry.'

I could scream at the languid cop, but I kept my voice under control so he wouldn't hang up on me. 'I know someone was coming. He's here. But he's unconscious. I need more help.'

'Madame, someone is coming to help you. Do not worry. Are you in danger? Is someone attacking you?'

At last, some sensible questions. Though the officer still sounded uninterested, I thought it prudent to answer him. 'No, I'm in an empty office.'

'Fine. Stay there. Lock the door if you can. I will stay on the line until my colleague arrives.'

What good would that do me? 'No, thank you. I have to go and take care of your colleague.' I hung up in frustration, looking around for something that might revive Chagrin. The bottles on the file cabinet were labelled bleach and rubbing alcohol. Neither seemed useful in this case. A foul-smelling cloth was on the floor next to Chagrin's head. It made me queasy, so I dumped it in the waste paper basket and put that on the other side of the room.

Now what? As I stared at the fallen major, I contemplated my options. Staying in this office would be the not-stupid thing to do *if* I could be sure help was on the way. But I was still half convinced the officer on the phone had meant Chagrin was on his way here.

I tried calling Jacqueline again but wasn't surprised there was no answer. If she'd seen her phone, she would have called me back by now. But the unconscious cop in Franck's office could only mean one thing: Beau *was* in danger. Franck had already made clear he didn't care about their familial bond. If he was now knocking out cops and leaving them lying in his office, he probably didn't care too much about anything any more.

I glanced at the computer screen, lit up by another flash of lightning. Would Franck still use the same password he'd had all those years ago? He didn't know I knew it then, so he might not have had reason to change it. His computer could perhaps provide evidence of the size of his debt. That might give me an idea of the lengths Franck would go to in order to settle it.

Then again, he might use a different password on his work laptop. And I didn't have time to go trawling through emails and documents in hopes of finding something incriminating when Franck could be planning to end his nephew's life right now.

Swallowing, I peered through the narrow window, but it only showed me the door opposite. I opened the door and sneaked out of the office into the empty corridor, tiptoeing away from the stairs leading to the front office and listening at each of the doors for any sound at all, but by the time I'd reached the end of the corridor, I'd heard nothing. One final door at the end led to the factory floor below. The glass pane gave me a clear view of the gleaming stainless steel vats and pipes beyond, but I hesitated getting closer, as anyone on the other side would also have a clear view of me.

Slowly approaching the door, I stretched my neck to check out as much of the factory as I could without being too obvious, but the area seemed abandoned. Since there were no employees present apart from the lady at the front desk, none of the machines were working either, so I gathered up my courage and opened the door.

He was here. That unpleasant tingle at the back of my neck had not failed me yet. The sound of the rain on the metal roof was louder here than it had been in the offices, which helped mask the sound of my hard-soled heels on the metal staircase. Scanning my surroundings for movement, I descended as quietly as I could. Stacks of cardboard boxes, plastic containers, and barrels of chemicals provided plenty of hiding places for me as I moved around the floor, rounding all sorts of machines that would ordinarily be producing, filling, and packing anything to do with household cleaning. An interesting olfactory mix of engine grease and soap entered my nostrils and made my nose tingle.

Don't. Sneeze. Sneezing would be just about the worst thing I could do right now. Apart from my phone ringing, maybe. I reached into my purse and set my phone to silent, just in case.

Then I heard a door open to my left. I ducked behind a softly humming vat and shuffled nearer, keeping so low my petticoat trailed over the floor.

'They'll know it was you.'

Beau was here! And not unconscious, like Chagrin. Was that good or bad? If Franck had knocked out a policeman, did he still consider Beau an ally?

'Knowing and proving are two different things,' Franck's voice answered. He grunted, then I heard a dull thunk, like a heavy object being moved.

'Like everyone knows it was you who killed Seive?'

Franck panted. 'How could it have been? I was at my dear wife's hotel.'

'Ex-wife.'

Franck laughed. 'I knew you couldn't be trusted. But' – another grunt and another thunk – 'I can take care of that problem too, now. Very efficient. I like that.'

My stomach turned. What was he planning? I'd made it to a machine consisting mostly of tubes and cables. As long as I kept myself still, I could now see Franck without being seen. A door with a big piratey sticker of a skull and crossbones on it was propped open behind him, and he was lugging boxes onto the factory floor.

Beau's voice came from the right, and I carefully moved to get a view of him. He was standing with his back to me, on the other side of the tubey machine. His arms were up, and when my gaze followed his pose, I could just see a glint of packing tape around his wrists when it was lit up by the lightning outside. Thunder followed more quickly now.

'Capucine likes it too, I imagine,' he said.

Franck paused, dumping another box after a second or two and coming closer. I made myself as small as I could, leaning back on my high heels and wishing I'd worn kittens.

'You mentioned her this morning. Who is she?'

'She's a pretty good actress too. Had me convinced she hated you. Did you teach her?'

Franck only put his hands on his hips. I wanted to warn Beau. No good ever came from Franck putting his hands on his hips. But Beau was probably already aware of the threat, seeing as he was tied up. I eyed the tape again, which had been wrapped around one of the tubes. Could I somehow free Beau without being seen? On my own, I was no match for Franck, but together, we could definitely take him.

'But now I know you two are in this together,' Beau continued.

Franck shrugged and returned to the boxes, ripping one open. 'Knowing and proving are two different things,' he repeated. 'And after your tragic demise, no one will even know.'

'I told Julie.'

My eyes widened and my heart beat more quickly at the mention of my name, as if it alone could reveal my crouching presence.

Taking a little pot out of the box, Franck laughed again. How I hated that sound. Franck only ever laughed in derision. Mostly of me. I had been free of it for years, but here I was again, cowering, hearing him laugh at my expense. I squeezed my eyes shut as he uttered the words I knew were coming.

'Julie! What good is that going to do you? All she ever thinks about is what colour to wear and how to sell people stuff that's supposed to make your skin glow. What's in it, radium?' He laughed again at his own joke while my lip wobbled.

Looking good makes people feel good. He never understood how important that is. But even knowing he was wrong, his words still hurt. They took me right back to that horrid apartment we'd shared after he'd driven away everyone I cared about.

I am a strong woman. Franck does not rule my life any more. I took a deep breath and repeated the words to myself until I believed at least the first part once more. The second part was hard to convince myself of, as I was cowering a few feet away from him. No, not cowering. Hiding. No, also not that. Biding my time. Better.

Opening my eyes once more, I glanced up. If I stood on the metal boxy bit with the buttons currently digging into my knee, I should just about be able to reach through the jungle of tubes and cables to the tape holding Beau's hands. But there was no way I could pull it loose. He'd been tugging on it and the plastic had formed a thick rope that the nail file I'd been hoping to use was no match for.

Franck had been typing on a flip phone. That must be the one Beau had seen him use before. Only now did I remember Franck scrolling on a smartphone when he was at the hotel. Another clue I should have picked up on if I weren't so distracted by Franck being... well, Franck. And now that I saw the flip phone, I remembered its twin at Capucine's house. I'd never even wondered how she could answer video calls on that. How could I have been so blind?

'All right. Just in case Julie has some sort of brain wave and decides to act on your information.' He waved the phone in front of him. 'Taken care of.' He turned back to the boxes, unpacking more of the pots.

I took the opportunity to climb onto the switch box, navigate between the machine's cables, and stretch towards Beau's wrists. Reaching as far as I could, I touched the tape binding them with my fingertips, but there were no loose ends to pull. Feeling around, I noticed the tape was wound around only one of the tubes, which ran horizontally towards me for a few inches before disappearing into another metal box, fastened by a heavy bolt. The bolt felt sturdy, but at least it was within my reach. A jolt of optimism gave me the strength to undo it, but when I tugged at the cable, it didn't come loose. I tugged harder, but because it was connected on Beau's side of the box, it was too far away from me to get a good grip.

Contemplating my next move, I checked on Franck. He was opening pots and emptying them on the floor. Little round pellets scattered everywhere.

'If they find me tied up, they'll know it wasn't an accident.' Beau's voice was getting a strain to it I could understand. So far, no police had shown up.

In my purse, my phone started to buzz. Hoping it was Jacqueline, I took it out, but Capucine's name flashed on the screen. I wrinkled my nose and put the phone back, but seeing her name had pushed my brain to make a strange connection, and I took off my heel. Stretching up again, I hooked it around the cable and pulled with all my might. The cable shot loose, and I staggered back, hitting the floor with a painful blow, but I smiled proudly at my ingenuity.

'I wish you hadn't hidden that key.'

Franck's voice was too close. A wave of fear washed over me as I looked up at the man standing next to me, his hands on his hips. Lightning lit him from behind, and the accompanying thunder made his dark silhouette seem transported straight from my nightmares.

I could only whisper, 'What key?'

24
That was for him

'I think he means this one.'

'Léon!'

If there was one person I did not expect to see, it was my amazing economics professor. But there he was, accompanied by Jacqueline and Brigadier-Chef Rouletabille, who held on to Capucine. Léon held up his hand, a simple key dangling from a cord.

Franck had whipped around at the unexpected sound of Léon's voice and was now gawping at the key, following its gentle swaying with his eyes. 'How...'

'I found it wedged behind the radiator when I stayed with Julie a few months ago.' He turned to me. 'I forgot to give it to you and somehow it ended up in my suitcase. You never mentioned missing it, so I left it in my luggage for when I came back. When you called two days ago, upset and scared, I suddenly realised the key I found wasn't yours. I didn't want to burden you with any more fears, but I changed to an earlier flight and informed Jacqueline. I'm sorry, my love, perhaps I should have told you, but you were already so distraught. I only wanted you to calm down and sleep, not worry about getting me involved.'

All over my body, my skin was tingling. My hero had come to save me! Of course, I'd already saved my assistant so he could do the saving for me, but still. I loved this man so much!

Beau stepped out from behind the machine, ripping the tape off his wrists and rubbing them. Franck gave him a sideways glance, then staggered backwards against the metal of the tubey machine as Beau's fist met his chin. Beau continued balling the tape as if nothing had happened, but when Franck straightened, Beau punched him again.

Both Jacqueline and Rouletabille moved to step in, but Beau held up both hands in peace. 'That was for him.' He pointed at Léon, who tried and failed to hide a grin.

By this point, I had moved safely away from my ex to hold the hand of my true love. Franck's gears were visibly turning, but even he could see no way out of this one. When Rouletabille approached him, but he sidestepped him and kissed Capucine, however, I almost keeled over.

Léon squeezed my hand, but Beau gave a grim smile. 'Oh, you hadn't figured that one out?'

'But... he can't... I mean, he never... How?' What I meant to say was that I knew they were in it together, but I had considered Franck incapable of love. Manipulation was his game. He would make you think anything you wanted until he got what *he* wanted, and then he'd be done with you. Or worse. But right now, he got what he definitely did not want, and still he showed affection. This did not add up at all.

As Rouletabille put Franck in handcuffs, Capucine addressed me. 'When I said I was sorry, back in your dressing room, I meant it. I *had* never thought about you in all our planning. You were just Franck's ex, no more than a cog in the machine, a woman I'd never met but assumed I wouldn't like just because he hated you.'

I didn't reply. Was she saying she liked me? Despite using me in the most despicable way? Seeing Franck arrested to be locked away – again, but this time for a good while longer – should have made me feel relieved. In a way, it did, or I knew it would very soon, but I was still reeling from that kiss.

'You're different from Franck. That was exciting to him at first, but she's the same. You can't compare the two.' Beau shrugged. 'You're better off not understanding.'

For one fleeting moment I was in awe of his wisdom, but Léon pulled me against him and I forgot everything else.

-oOo-

Rain crashed against the window of the white villa that in this light looked more grey. The depressing hue was only enhanced by the strong men removing the last bits of expensive furniture from Sandrine's home. I came to stand next to her at the window as the men started their truck and drove off.

'Is there anything else I can do?' I asked softly.

She wrapped her arms around herself and took a deep breath. Then she smiled. Not the sad, brave smile I'd expected, but a truly radiant beam. It almost made me recoil. Her husband had been arrested for fraud, and all her possessions taken away to pay the fine. How could she possibly be happy?

'I know,' Sandrine said, holding up a calming hand, 'it's strange. But I much prefer to be living in that tiny studio in town, waiting for Emile to return an honest man, than to stay here and pretend that I don't know something's off. Pretend I fit in with Apolline and her crowd. Pretend that the villains coming over are legitimate businessmen. That's not the kind of acting I like.'

I gave her a small smile. We both had had a lot to process in the last few days. But whereas I now had Léon to fall back on, Sandrine's rock had been taken away. 'Mislabelling' was the term for it. When Emile had learned the vicomtesse used Pinot Noir grapes in some of her wines, he'd started selling them under different, very expensive, labels.

It had been quite a shock to learn that Sebastian Tombs was an undercover agent from Interpol, looking for evidence against Emile. According to Sandrine, it had started as a bit of an adventure, seeing how far he could push this new endeavour, but when Ronan Kelly became involved, the whole thing quickly got out of hand. When Sebastian found his evidence and came to arrest Emile, he'd confessed everything to his wife, saying how sorry he was and begging her not to leave him. But that had been the furthest thing from Sandrine's mind. After the stock value of Emile's legal ventures tanked, too, she'd found herself a new place to live and arranged for the sale of everything that did not hold emotional value to her. All she kept were some clothes and her wedding ring.

'If there's anything I can do for you, let me know,' I said, taking her hand. 'Give me a chance to return your kindness.' Though I was still working through some of the issues Franck's actions had initiated, I'd wanted to be here for Sandrine the same way she'd been there for me.

She laughed. 'That's nothing. You almost ended up in the middle of *my* troubles too. Your whole story about the lights in the night only made sense after Emile was arrested. Ronan had been planning to take over the whole business, so you and Beau actually did us a favour.'

Shaking my head, I smiled back. 'Emile did himself the favour.' The expensive bottle of Pinot Noir he'd given us was a fake. It contained Emile's own Beaujolais wine under a counterfeit label. Ronan had got rid of all the other evidence, but Sebastian had seen the bottle change hands and come to us to ask if he could 'borrow' it. Turns out that was exactly what Emile had hoped would happen.

The light signals that had kept me up were meant for Ronan. Looking back, I wondered how I ever could have suspected Beau to be involved. He'd told me later that he'd found the chair in the corridor empty, but the throw on top was still warm. If he'd come out seconds earlier, he might have solved the whole thing right there and then. Ronan had claimed to know nothing of any sordid deals, but he'd been sloppy and left a paper trail.

With Sebastian in possession of the evidence, both Ronan and Emile would go to jail, but to his more unsavoury contacts, Emile could maintain that he had not willingly given up the game. That would hopefully ensure his safety once he was released.

Sandrine smiled her gratitude.

'So, are you coming to my garden party?' I asked to lighten the mood. A particularly strong blast of wind thrashed the rain against the window right then, and we both burst out laughing.

25

And so, Blondie, it's goodbye

Jacqueline squeezed me in the tightest hug. 'I'm going to miss you so much. Who else is going to bring me dead bodies and villains to catch?'

'You can always join the force in America.'

Ken shook his blond locks. 'Nuh-uh. No.'

We both laughed. Sipping the champagne left over from my party, we were gathered together in my garden, a week after Franck and Capucine had been arrested. I had decided I needed another party, a real one, to drive away the memory of the last. Léon was back, Franck was arrested. Those were good reasons on their own, but the fact that both Jacqueline and Beau – *and* Céline – were leaving brought a sad tinge to the festivities. At least they were going away on a high. I'd make sure of that with this party.

Dumping the stylish decorations from my disastrous promotional party, I'd gone the other direction and bought bunting, balloons, streamers, and lanterns in every colour of the rainbow. The food matched my colourful theme, and as it turned out, Beau's best friend Gío was a trained bartender, mixing up the most glorious concoctions.

I'd invited everyone I knew, even Chantelle. I'd almost only invited her to tease Beau, but even he had to admit I would need a new assistant now that he'd be gone. He'd been practically glued to Céline for a week, meaning she'd basically moved in above my studio, though I hardly ever saw them. Of course, I had my own guest to occupy myself with.

Léon moved among the partygoers with ease, as if he'd known them forever. *Maman* adored him. Even David seemed to like him, but this I had to hear from Maëline. They'd all met him before, of course, but now that he'd announced he'd be staying in France because he wanted to be close to me, they took our relationship more seriously.

I had been on cloud nine, trying not to plan too much but really building castles in the air. Now, seeing everyone's smiling faces around me, my rose-coloured glasses were pretty much a hot pink. Not even the presence of Anne-Bonny, who was filming herself in front of my pool dressed in a white bikini with blue plastic sun visors over her boobs, could darken my happiness. After Franck's arrest, I'd gathered up the courage to ask her about her connection to Cyprien. He had disappeared off the map completely, and neither the police nor Beau's family could find him, so I thought I'd try my one lead. I'd seen

Anne-Bonny talk to Cyprien just before Beau was shot, but she had no idea who I was talking about.

Then again, she'd been a little distracted at the time. She'd come to the door with a pile of shredded fabric in her arms. When I asked if that was the latest trend, she'd almost burst into tears, raging about a cat getting trapped in her closet. I commiserated but that night, I'd put out a dish of the extra stinky fishy food Henri loved so much.

Maile, not wanting to steal the limelight, had confided in me that I was going to be a godmother. She knew this would make me practically burst with the inner battle between aching to tell everyone her secret and wanting to be the heart of my own party, but even that I magnanimously forgave her with a teary hug.

Instead, I imagined myself a few years from now, joining Marie and her little ones, who were playing with the children of Sophia Labouche in my pool. This godchild of mine would be the cutest, most amazing of them all. She – or he – would—

'I still don't understand,' Nienke said, joining me and my mother at the edge of the pool. 'I thought you said she hated him.'

I nodded slowly while she slurped a bright orange cocktail. 'That's what Capucine led me to believe. She was so convincing, playing on my own experiences and on what I'd heard from former clients when she told me about being scammed.

But in fact, when Franck had tried to scam her, she admired his handiwork and offered him a partnership. When Franck and I were married, I never heard of her. She was basically a colleague, and Franck never introduced me to any of his shady contacts, though I didn't know they were shady at the time. When he went to prison, she went back to legitimate deals for a while, but they stayed in touch and fell in love.'

I had to suppress the urge to retch. I still couldn't fathom the kind of character that Franck would fall in love with. Beau had probably come closest when he said she was the same. He'd fallen in love with his own mirror. Now that did make sense.

I sighed. 'Apparently, prison did nothing to mellow his feelings towards me. When it became clear that his creditors would want their money the moment he was free, he had to come up with the cash quickly. But in all that time, his cronies hadn't been able to find the key to his precious safe deposit box. He'd hidden it in my great-aunt's house, but it wasn't there any more, so he couldn't get to his money unless he robbed the bank. But getting me to hand over the key seemed like less trouble. Only problem was, I had no idea there had been a key to begin with.'

'And neither did I, even though I'd found it.' Léon was one of several people who had joined the group and were now listening to my explanation. Most of them had only heard snippets of the story, so they were hanging on my every word.

I swirled my *rosé pamplemousse*, prolonging my moment. 'Franck, however, did not believe that. While he had to start thinking of different ways he might pay off his creditors, he kept trying to put pressure on me so I would deliver the key to his illegitimate fortune. He set up a scheme to take over from Beau's father, Patrick, with the aid of Michel Seive. Seive, however, saw a chance to better himself, so Franck was forced to take him out of the equation. It secured his relationship with Patrick, who gave him back his high-paying job at the factory, but it meant he now had blood on his hands, even if he was only the guy giving the order.'

I popped an olive in my mouth and chewed demurely before continuing, relishing the impatience of my audience. 'Capucine, meanwhile, had her own problems. She had once been married—'

'Ooh, yes, I found that out,' Jessica Rose interrupted with shiny eyes. She looked around the group gathered under the big, white parasol. 'Alain knew her casually, so I asked around his hoity-toity friends. They had plenty to say! Nothing was ever proven, but there were rumours that she'd married him for his money and then helped him along, so to speak. He was old.'

'Well, there's proof now,' Joseph Rouletabille said. I'd invited the policeman because I liked him. He took me seriously. But not too much so, as I found out. 'Contrary to what you might think when you hear Julie speak, the police do actually do some work. Since nobody could provide us with motive and we were at first unable to locate any family, we searched Delphine Montpertuis's home and found a treasure trove of secrets. Other people's secrets. It took us some time sorting the less serious from the ones people might kill to keep, but it did lead us to keep an eye on Capucine Jamin.'

'Sadly, this was after she'd torched Cyprien's car with Seive's body in it,' I said, bringing the attention back to me. 'Franck and Capucine had worked out a scheme in which they would each get rid of the other's problem, and because their relationship was unknown to anyone but Cyprien, they might be prime suspects, but would have rock solid alibis.'

'Both of those alibis being you,' Beau added. 'Franck always could hold a grudge. He'd been talking about revenge for months. Just when I thought he'd finally let go, he killed Delphine instead. I always knew it was him.'

I nodded, raising my glass to him. 'You did. I should have listened to you, but there was no evidence. As they'd predicted, without any direct link between Franck and Delphine, there was no proof the killer was anyone but an unknown burglar.'

'But why the shoe?' Marie Madora asked, the sugared violets dripping off her forgotten cake as the buttercream melted.

'Symbolic. Beau was right again with that. Franck resented that my fashion obsession, as he called it, was now making me a lot of money. Especially since he had money trouble. But he couldn't take mine the way he'd done before, so he thought of another way to traumatise me. I would be the perfect, reliable alibi. Everyone knew there was no chance I'd be on Franck's side, so if *I* said he couldn't be the killer, it must be true.'

Alain lifted his expensive, mirrored sunglasses to give me a puzzled look. 'But you only met her that morning. How could they know you would be their alibi?'

I cast down my gaze. This part of the plan I found truly devious. 'They relied on Franck's understanding of my character. He told Capucine that I "need people". Keeping people away from me had been his best tactic in keeping me obedient before. If they arranged for Capucine to have the stall next to Céline's, and Capucine could be graceful and friendly, I was bound to invite her into my circle.'

And I had. This had been my biggest struggle over the past week. Was I that predictable? Was I so dependent on other people that I threw the doors wide open to bad influences? Léon had had his work cut out for him in convincing me that being open and welcoming was not a negative trait. That I couldn't possibly have predicted someone would abuse it in such a horrific manner. I was doing my best to accept his reasoning but I had a way to go.

Beau took a pull from his beer bottle. Fancy drinks were wasted on him. 'Capucine and Franck communicated through an email address they could both access, making sure to delete their browser history afterwards. For any casual observer, there was no link between them. After a few weeks of not seeing each other, though, Franck bought them both a burner phone, supposedly for emergencies. But they couldn't help sending each other messages throughout the day. And so what was supposed to be a hidden relationship was starting to leave traces.'

Céline squeezed her arm around his waist, and he stopped his story to kiss her. Again. I refrained from rolling my eyes, which I thought very grown-up of myself, and picked up where he left off.

'Delphine had threatened to go to the police with her evidence on Capucine's earlier crime – the "helping along" of her husband – and she wanted to be paid. But not just with money. She enjoyed taking things people valued. One of those things was a ring with a big yellow gemstone that Delphine wore to my party. However, when we went to talk to Capucine afterwards, she was wearing that ring. The only way she could have got it back was from the killer, so that was the first real clue we had that she was involved in Delphine's murder.

'Franck had taken care of her problem. Now she had to help him with his. Cyprien had already done the hard bit of actually killing Seive, but they still had a body to get rid of. With Franck under my watchful eye, and Cyprien so obviously tailing someone that he had to have been noticed, neither could be the one driving Cyprien's car to a field just within sight of a vineyard where people were picking grapes and setting it on fire. They used a…' I fluttered my lashes at Léon. 'Help me out with the big words?'

'Pyrophoric substance.'

'That. Some sort of potent… hydra?'

'Potassium hydride.'

Wasn't he brilliant? 'Yes. It comes in little balls of wax, but ignites when it comes into contact with air. Franck took it from the factory because it's used in the manufacture of some cleaning products. Leaving it in a car in a heatwave meant the wax melted and the potassium stuff would take care of the rest. Capucine, wearing Franck's clothes, would be long gone by the time the car caught alight, but it would burn with such a high heat that all evidence would be destroyed before the fire brigade could get to it. And nobody would associate Capucine with the fire. Someone from the Rich Women Club had seen her, but she got her times mixed up, so we dismissed her statement, and with it any evidence that Capucine might have been at the scene.

'Franck was going to use the same chemical to set fire to the factory. He needed money more quickly than he could get it from Patrick, so he was hoping to get his hands on the insurance money. He'd already changed the beneficiary, and again, the fire would be hot enough to destroy any evidence that Beau had been tied up and Chagrin knocked out with some home-made chloroform. It was quite clever, actually.'

'But they hadn't counted on you,' Léon said with some pride in his voice that made me giddy. 'He's not some criminal mastermind. He's just a narcissistic man who chose the wrong person to intimidate.'

I blushed, recalling all the despair I'd poured on him the past week about knowing what a terrible person Franck was and yet still falling for his lies again. Having the support of this good man was more than I could have asked for.

Beau raised his glass to me. 'He should have realised how formidable you are.'

My colour deepened. I was the centre of attention at my own party, and I was loving every minute. Especially now I knew Franck couldn't possibly ruin this one.

At the end of the afternoon, my guests returned home one by one. Tiana and Lucas started clearing up the dishes, while I joined Sandrine at the edge of the pool. 'How are you feeling?'

She gave me the sad smile I'd expected a few days earlier. 'A bit lonely, to be honest. But also relieved, still. I had everything money can buy, and I'm happier living in a tiny apartment. Well, I will be once Emile joins me.' She perked up, holding up the dregs of a blue drink with a parasol and a skewer full of fruit. 'Meanwhile, I've landed a part in a television show! I'm starting next week.'

'That's amazing! Well done!' I gave Sandrine a hug before she, too, left.

I reclined on one of the sun chairs, letting the late afternoon sun caress my legs while I kept my head in the shade of the parasol. Silently, I thanked my Great-Aunt Géraldine for the wonderful house I now called my own. In the year I'd lived here, I'd amassed so many good memories that the recent horror was already fading. It would be a while before I could cross my courtyard without thinking back to what had happened, but when I'd passed this morning, Henri had stretched himself out in the shade at exactly the spot that haunted my dreams. I'd spent some time imprinting the view of Henri over the image in my mind and I was confident it would stay in place, at least for a while.

My house. My pool. My soon-to-be-ex assistant, whom I could now unreservedly call my friend. And the love of my life, who'd recovered my ex's fortune and redistributed it among his victims. Not his creditors. Franck could deal with that in another twenty years. Perhaps I shouldn't be vindictive about that, but life felt pretty good right now.

Beau, his arms full of wrapping paper, passed behind my chair. 'Everything all right, my queen?'

I waved a regal hand. 'Blondie, as long as you don't call me your deer, your chick, or your shrimp, I am going to let that remark pass.'

Céline handed me a glass of champagne with a grin. I really shouldn't but accepted nonetheless.

'You're invited,' she told me, and I winked in answer.

'Are we having a party too?' Beau asked, dumping his load of paper in the recycling bin.

'You will,' Léon answered as he lowered himself on the chair beside me and took my hand.

I sighed. 'And so, Blondie, it's goodbye.'

THE END

Other books by Christa Bakker

<u>*Other books in this series:*</u>

Death by Naked Ladies

Beaujolais Blood

The Cold Case: a Vintage Murder

Sieste in Peace

The Gift of Death

Second Hand Murder

Sign up for a FREE Christmas story at

<u>https://christabakker.com/newsletter</u>

Acknowledgements

Though this is the last book in this series, my gratitude to you, the reader will never stop. I love that you've read all the way to here! I hope you, like me, are a little sad to say goodbye to these characters, but don't worry! There are plenty more to come. I'm sure you'll fall in love with them just as much.

As always, my editor, Kristen Tate, has made this book what it is now, and I couldn't be happier with her work!

Thank you to my first readers, my mother and author Carole Marples, for giving me precious feedback on everything that was wrong with earlier drafts.

My love and thanks to my husband, and to my children, who have both had roles in my stories. Happy now?

Editing by Kristen Tate at The Blue Garret

Book cover by Erik & Christa Bakker

1st edition 2025

ISBN: 978-1-916998-17-9

Visit the author's website at: www.christabakker.com